Chapter 1

When the other guests left after the dinner party, the two women sat on in the living room while Sarah's husband cleared up in the kitchen, whistling cheerfully.

She grinned at her cousin as they sat in the living room were saying goodbye at the door. 'You always look magnificent when you're angry, Megan. It really is true about red hair and tempers, isn't it?'

'My hair is auburn!' Megan snapped automatically. 'And you're not going to distract me with that old line. You promised faithfully! No more introductions, you said.'

Sarah's voice became coaxing. 'You're nearly thirty now. Surely you want to get married and to do that, you have to find a man. So you need to meet more people and –'

'I'm twenty-eight. And not quite on my last legs yet.' Megan glared at her cousin. 'It's not a sin to be single, you know.'

'No, but it's natural to want a husband and family, and besides, I've watched you cuddling my little Amy. You're getting quite mumsy. But how are you going to meet any decent guys if you will go on living in Upper Shenstead? Why, you didn't even move to London when you were offered a fabulous job there two years ago.'

'I didn't move up to London because I prefer to live in the country.'

Sarah wrinkled her nose and blew out a scornful puff of air. 'Yeah, well, let's face it, love, you are a bit of a stick-in-the-mud.'

For a moment Megan nearly rose to the bait, then she got herself under control. 'That's my choice. You just butt out of my love life from now on.' She stood up. 'Good night and thanks for a truly ghastly evening.'

She was out of the house and unlocking her car before Sarah caught up with her.

'I only do it because I care about you.'

Megan waved but didn't answer.

As she left the busy little town behind and headed back to her village, she wondered why she'd got so over-the-top mad at her cousin tonight. After all, Sarah had been trying to find her a husband for years. So what had changed?

She answered that ruefully as she parked her car and opened the garden gate. What had changed was herself. She'd started to feel restless and look at friends' children enviously.

Sarah was right about one thing: it was more than time to make some changes in her life, which was partly why she'd applied to emigrate to Australia. But to her disappointment, they'd rejected her. Secretaries, even those with top skills, were not in great demand down under, it seemed.

So she'd have to think of something else. Only what? She definitely didn't want to live in a city.

And for all her fiery words, she did want to get married and have a family - and sooner rather than later. If she could meet someone who . . . she sighed. Perhaps she was too picky.

No. As far as she was concerned, marriage was for life and she wasn't getting into it until she knew the man was right for her.

The following week Megan took Friday off work and set out for Northumberland, humming as she drove along. She took it easy and was glad when she left the motorway.

This was an important trip. She'd decided to make changes and facing the ghosts from the past seemed the right first step to sort out her life. She'd lived in the north-east as a child and never been back since her parents were killed in an accident. But she remembered it. Oh, yes. And dreamed about it.

Just north of Newcastle the engine of her car coughed, faltered, then picked up again. She listened apprehensively, but nothing else happened, so she carried on.

As she left Morpeth behind, however, the car began to jerk and slow down. 'Oh, no! Don't do this to me!' she begged, but the engine died completely and the car coasted gently to a halt by the side of the road.

She lifted the bonnet, but could see nothing obviously wrong. To her relief there was a garage a couple of hundred yards away, so she didn't bother to ring for roadside assistance, but trudged towards it.

They were about to close, but towed her car in and the mechanic gave it a cursory examination. 'Looks like a couple of hours' work there. I can do it for you tomorrow afternoon.'

She stared at him in dismay. 'Oh, no! I'm on holiday. I was going up to Alnwick.'

He shrugged. 'I'd normally work late, but I've got an important family party to attend tonight in Newcastle. Look, if you want somewhere to stay, there's a country house hotel just down the road. I can drop you and your luggage off there on my way home. Best I can offer.'

She didn't have much choice, did she? Sighing, Megan collected her things from the car, feeling annoyed at how her precious weekend break was turning out.

If this had been a romance novel, the mechanic would have been a hunk and would have invited her out to dinner.

Life wasn't like that. The man was fifty if he was a day, and rather chubby.

Pity.

Ben noticed the woman as she walked into Reception because she was radiating suppressed anger and looked magnificent. She had long, curly auburn hair cascading down her back, a vivid fact and nice legs. His eyes lingered on the legs. Very nice.

She was probably part of the damned conference, though. People had been pouring into this hotel for the last hour, shouting greetings to one another and disrupting the peace of the foyer bar. If he'd known how crowded The Ashington would be, he'd have gone elsewhere. Maybe he would move on tomorrow.

As he turned towards the lift, a man bumped into him. He heard a voice call out and next minute he was shoved out of the way as someone pounded past him. 'What the - '

He spun round to see the auburn-haired woman a few yards away, struggling with a young man who managed to free one hand and take a swing at her.

Ben dragged the guy off her, not sure what was happening.

'Don't let him go! He just took your wallet!' she gasped. 'I saw him put it in his pocket.'

A burly concierge came up in time to hear this. 'Let me.' He was strong enough to hold the young fellow still while he felt in the jacket pocket and produced two wallets. 'Not many people carry two of these.'

'The top one's mine,' Ben said.

The thief made a sudden lunge and nearly got away, but the woman tripped him up. The concierge hauled him to his feet, keeping a firmer hold this time, helped by Ben.

By this time a crowd had gathered. A man in a dark suit came up to them and said in a low voice, 'I'm the Duty Manager. Shall we deal with this in my office?' He gestured towards the right.

'I've got him now.' The concierge frog-marched the thief towards the door.

Ben turned to the young woman, who was rubbing her temple where the man had punched her. 'Are you all right?'

'Yes. Luckily it was just a glancing blow.' She glanced towards the reception desk. 'I'd better get my luggage.'

'I'll fetch it for you.' Ben strode across the foyer, looked back to confirm that he had the right things, then brought them across and escorted her to the manager's office.

Inside the office, the young man was standing with arms folded. 'She stole the wallet and planted it on me,' he said immediately.

Ben glared at him. 'She couldn't have done. I watched her walk in and cross to Reception. She was still standing there when you bumped into me.'

He turned back to her. 'I can't thank you enough. I'd have lost my wallet but for you.' There was a bruise forming on her forehead, but otherwise she looked more exhilarated than upset. Her air of fresh vigour appealed to Ben. Very much.

She smiled. 'You're welcome. I hope he hasn't given me a black eye, though.'

'No, just a bruise on the forehead. About there. He touched his own in the same place. 'Are you sure you're all right?'

'I'm fine.'

'Not many women would have tackled him.'

She shrugged. 'I've done a bit of self-defence. I went after him automatically.'

'It was a brave thing to do, and we're very grateful,' the manager said approvingly.

Megan could feel herself flushing as all four men stared at her. 'It's nothing, honestly. Anyone would have done the same thing.'

'I doubt it.' The stranger's gaze was still warm.

She took a deep breath, or tried to. Now that the incident was over, reaction had set in and she felt flustered and uncertain. This wasn't helped by standing next to the best-looking man she'd seen in a long time. She stole a glance sideways. He was more than good-looking. Heavens, he was downright handsome! Dark hair, straight nose, firm chin, broad shoulders - the works!

She caught sight of the clock. 'Is this going to take

long?' she asked the manager. 'I was just trying to book a room for tonight and you seem rather full. My car's broken down.'

He picked up the phone, had a quiet conversation, then smiled benevolently at her. 'We are pretty full, but there is a spare suite. You can have that. And the hotel will not, of course, charge you for your accommodation tonight, Miss - ?'

'Ross. Megan Ross.'

He turned back to relay her name to the person on the other end of the phone, then nodded to the concierge. 'Could you have Miss Ross's luggage taken up to Number 36, please, Jeff, while we sort this out? Now, Mr Saunders, I think I'd better hold on to your wallet till the police arrive. Perhaps you'd like to take a seat.'

'I'll sit near the door.' He stared at the thief, who scowled back at him.

'And I'll keep watch this side,' the manager said.

As they waited, Megan wondered how much a suite normally cost, but didn't like to ask. Whatever. She was relieved to have somewhere to stay and it'd be another new experience staying in a suite. Wait till she told Sarah!

It was a while before the police arrived, by which time Megan, sitting on the couch, had memorised every inch of Ben Saunders' face and noted that he had shapely hands. She'd felt him staring at her, as well, and had tried not to react to that.

She must look a mess. Her clothes were crumpled from the journey, her hair clasp must have fallen out in the struggle, and it felt as if her hair had reverted to its usual wild tangle. She tried surreptitiously to smooth it down, saw Ben watching her, so left it alone, because she'd read somewhere that women fiddled with their hair when they were attracted to a man.

She sighed. Well, she was attracted. Who wouldn't be? Why couldn't she have met a man like this when she was looking her best?

The police officer was shown in, recognised the would-be thief on sight and chuckled. 'Not you again!'

Although the young guy stopped protesting his innocence and admitted to the attempted theft, it was still quite a while before the paperwork was completed. Only then were Megan and Ben allowed to leave.

As they came out of the office into the foyer, he turned to smile at her. 'You must let me show my gratitude by buying you dinner. Your quick action's saved me a lot of hassles.'

'There's no need. I was happy to help.' Not that she'd mind having dinner with him. He was every young woman's fantasy come true. But she didn't want him to take her to dinner out of cool gratitude. She moved across to the Reception desk to pick up her key, but glanced sideways in surprise when Ben Saunders followed her.

'We both have to eat,' he pointed out. 'It'd be silly for each of us to sit alone in the dining room.'

His smile made her breath catch in her throat. Perhaps she would have dinner with him, then. No, what was she thinking of? A man like him was bound to be married - they always were - and it was one of her prime rules not to get mixed up with married men. And actually, she didn't know the first thing about him and she always tried to be careful.

'I'd really enjoy some company,' he added quietly.

Well, give him a gold star for perseverance, whatever else. She hesitated, glancing towards his hand. No ring. But that didn't mean anything. Most men didn't wear wedding rings. Though she'd once or twice wished they were obliged to by law!

He chuckled as if he knew what she was thinking about. 'I'm not married or spoken for. And you'll be quite safe having dinner with a stranger in a busy hotel like this. Only we're not quite strangers now, are we?'

She gave up the battle to be sensible and smiled at him. 'Oh, well. If you're sure. I accept your kind offer.'

'I'm very sure. I'll pick you up in - what? Fifteen minutes?'

'Make it half an hour.'

That would give her time to smarten herself up - and calm down a bit. It was probably just reaction to the recent events that was making her heart beat so fast.

Who was she kidding? she admitted to herself as she stood beside him in the lift. You're reacting to him. And what normal woman wouldn't?

As she closed the door of her suite behind her, she leaned against it and let out her breath in a whoosh. Then she laughed aloud as she suddenly realised how far she'd stepped right out of her rut today. She'd headed back to lay her childhood ghosts, prevented a robbery and met a gorgeous man, who'd invited her to dinner.

Nothing would come of it - she'd never see him again after today - but just wait till she told Sarah about this little adventure!

She walked round the suite, enjoying the luxury. It was large and beautifully appointed, with a sitting room, bathroom, small kitchen and separate bedroom. She'd never have been to afford this, or rather, she'd never have spent as much money on one night's accommodation as this no doubt cost normally.

As she looked out of the window at tranquil formal gardens backed by a glorious sunset sky, her spirits lifted. There was nothing like a dash of luxury for lifting your spirits.

She unpacked rapidly, deciding to wear the new dress she'd fallen for last time she was in Cheltenham. She'd been in two minds as to whether to bring it. Thank goodness she had done! Half an hour wasn't nearly long enough to get ready, though. She tried two different hairstyles, then in desperation clipped her hair into a high knot of curls and teased a few strands out to soften her face.

Smoothing the dark green material of the dress over

her hips, she twisted round to see the side view. Life would, she thought for about the millionth time, be a lot easier if she didn't have such generous breasts. Her sort of curves had gone out with Marilyn Monroe. Thin was in these days, but she wasn't into starvation and a life on lettuce leaves

There was a knock on the door and she cast a last frantic glance in the mirror before opening it. Heavens, he was even more gorgeous than she'd remembered!

His eyes were warmly approving. 'You look lovely, Megan.'

'Oh. Well, um, thank you.' She never had known how to deal smoothly with compliments. Perhaps because her aunt and uncle weren't into lavish praise.

As she looked into his smoky grey eyes, the world receded for a moment and she could only stand there, trying to think of something casually confident to say - and failing. In fact, she couldn't think of a single word, let alone a whole string of them. Someone should put a blanket over her head and lead her away quietly.

She suddenly realised he'd said something else and was waiting for an answer. 'Sorry. I - um - didn't catch that.'

'I thought we might have a drink in the bar first.'

She nodded. 'That'd be lovely.'

But it was happy hour and the bar was full of noisy people who all seemed to know one another. He stopped in the doorway to scowl at them. 'It's like a madhouse in here and all the seats are taken anyway. Let's see if the restaurant is quieter.'

It was much quieter, but most of the space was taken up by some long tables set up but unoccupied. Presumably these were for the big group of revellers now occupying the bar.

'If I'd known there was a damned conference on,' he muttered. 'I'd never have come here. These country house hotels are usually quiet and comfortable.' His expression lightened slightly. 'On the other hand, if I hadn't come, I'd not have met you, and that'd be a pity.'

She blinked in surprise at this remark and looked at him doubtfully. Was he chatting her up, hoping to get lucky tonight? Because if so, he was going to be disappointed.

No, a man like him wouldn't be so crass, nor would he be short of female company.

The maître d'hôtel found them a table in a quiet corner and fussed over them in a way that surprised Megan. It was as if Ben was a celebrity. She studied him through narrowed eyes. If he was, she certainly didn't recognise his face.

He leaned back in his chair with a sigh, sounding tired. 'This is better. I hope you don't mind eating so early? I think we'd be wise to get our meal before the revellers take over in here as well.'

'I usually eat at six-thirty, so it suits me better, actually.' That's right, show him how unsophisticated you are!

'Great. I only had a scratch lunch and I'm starving. Shall we order?'

Once they were settled with glasses of wine, he asked casually, 'Do you make a habit of rescuing strangers like that?'

She wished he wouldn't go on about it. 'I've never rescued anyone from anything before. It was just a mad impulse. I hate thieves.'

'Well, I'm grateful for it.' His voice was understanding. 'And you don't want to talk about it any more. OK. Modesty rules. Tell me about yourself instead. What do you do for a living?'

He might as well know from the start how uninteresting her life was. 'I manage a suite of professional offices.'

'Do you enjoy doing that?'

She opened her mouth to say her usual yes, but what came out was, 'No. Not now, anyway. At first it was interesting, because I started out as a secretary and it was a step up. But it's no challenge any more.'

He gave her a quizzical glance. 'Then why do you continue?'

'Because it's the only reasonable job I can find near Upper Shenstead.' Well done! Emphasise the fact that you're a stick-in-the-mud, Megan! 'What do you do?'

'I've been working mostly in . . . er, real estate, but I've sold my business and I'm closing down a couple of other operations now.'

He sounded quite well off. Real hero material. 'What will you do next?'

'I'm not quite sure. Take a break till I've worked out what I want to do with my life for the next few years.'

'It must be wonderful to have a choice.'

A waiter brought her entrée and she stared down at it in anticipation. 'This is a work of art. It seems a pity to spoil the pretty patterns.' But she loved seafood, and one bite made her forget the elegant display and concentrate on the food, as he was doing.

A pianist appeared and sat down at the baby grand piano. She was good, too. Megan listened in pleasure as she ate. She hadn't enjoyed herself so much for ages.

When Ben asked her to dance, she went willingly into his arms, and though he held her in a light, easy grip, once again she was very aware of him and his firm body.

'I haven't been dancing for ages,' she said.

'You do it well.'

So did he. Unlike most men she'd danced with, he was leading her confidently round the small floor, avoiding other couples and still managing to maintain a conversation.

If only Sarah could see her now. Only, she couldn't pull out her mobile phone and ask a bystander to take a picture of them, so maybe her cousin wouldn't believe her about how attractive he was, how elegant this all felt.

Over the main course Megan inadvertently revealed her

interest in wildlife and the preservation of threatened species, something she didn't usually brandish in front of people. She found Ben well informed on the topic, not at all scornful like a couple of the guys Sarah had introduced her to.

In fact, their discussions all showed him to be a thinking man and they only stopped talking to eat.

By the time the dessert trolley was brought to their table, the restaurant was packed with the conference crowd, who were making a lot of noise.

He grimaced. 'They're only going to get worse as they get drunker, you know. Would you trust me enough to eat dessert in my suite?'

She stared at him in surprise, then a loud burst of laughter behind them was followed by several people whistling piercingly. 'Can we do that?'

He beckoned to the maître d'hôtel and within seconds Megan was following Ben out of the restaurant.

His room was an oasis of peace after the noisy restaurant, and it was even bigger than hers. She sighed in pleasure as she sank down on the sofa. 'That's better.'

He settled beside her, close but not too close, and began to rub his forehead.

'Headache?'

He nodded.

'Then maybe I should leave?'

He yawned, then looked at her wryly. 'Don't go yet. It's only jetlag. I was in New York two days ago.'

'Is it as wonderful as they say?'

'It's a pretty lively place. But I've had enough of cities. Which was why I booked in here. I fancied a few days of lazing around, going for long walks in the countryside.'

A knock on the door heralded the desserts they'd chosen. Megan's *spécialité de la maison* turned out to be two swans made of meringue swimming across a sea of apricot sauce, surrounded by pretty arrangements of exotic fruits. It vanished all too quickly and she looked up to find him yawning again.

She pushed her plate aside and stood up. 'I'd better go now. You look exhausted. Thank you so much for the dinner. It was delicious.'

To her disappointment, he didn't protest but rose with her and moved towards the door. Once there he took her in his arms. She'd been hoping all evening that he'd kiss her, though it couldn't lead anywhere, of course. She wasn't into one-night stands and they'd probably never meet again.

But still, a kiss could sweeten the memory.

This one didn't stay sweet for long. It went from gentle to passionate in about ten seconds flat. When he moved his lips away, it took her a minute to open her eyes.

Looking surprised, he let out his breath in a long, slow exhalation as he stared at her.

Was he going to kiss her again? She hoped so. But to her disappointment he stepped back a pace. She turned towards the door, determined not to betray how she felt.

'Will you spend tomorrow with me, Megan?'

She turned back, joy zipping through her. 'I'd like that. Though I'll have to check with the garage about when my car will be ready. What were you thinking of doing?'

'Flying to the moon, maybe, if you light my touch paper again.' He chuckled quietly. 'How about going for a nice long walk? You said you loved the countryside and I've had all too few chances to enjoy it in recent years. You can teach me about the local birdlife. Then lunch in a country pub, maybe, followed by a stroll on the nearest beach?'

'Sounds like my sort of day.'

He walked with her along the corridor to her room, waited until she'd opened the door, then nodded farewell. She couldn't resist lingering to watch him go.

A few paces away, he hesitated, then turned to ask, 'Breakfast at eight? Meet you in the restaurant?'

She nodded, closed the door and sagged against it,

beaming. He wanted to see her again. He really did.

Then, of course, she couldn't sleep, but started reliving the evening, thinking of witty remarks she could have made, but hadn't. She wished she had half his confidence and his easy way of dealing with people.

But even so, he did want to see her again. And she most definitely wanted to spend more time with him.

It's just a day out, she warned herself sternly. Don't read too much into it. Strangers meet, enjoy one another's company, spend a little time together, then go on their way.

But still . . . a man like him was such a boost for her morale.

She lay awake for a while, listening to the wind whining around the hotel. She couldn't help indulging in a few foolish fantasies, but who was to know about that?

All this after one kiss?

Chapter 2

When Megan drew back the curtains it was to see a misty landscape and rain hissing steadily against the windowpanes. She groaned in disappointment. 'Great day for a walk in the woods!' She went into the bathroom, feeling bitter about how life could give with one hand and take away with the other.

As she got out of the shower. Given the weather, the outing would be off, of course, so Ben would probably mile at her over breakfast, wish her well, then drive off into the mist.

When she went down to the restaurant, dressed in jeans and a sweater, she found Ben waiting, sipping a coffee and watching the door.

He greeted her with a rueful smile, waving one hand towards the windows. 'Just look at that weather! And the forecast is for more rain to come.'

Megan slipped into the chair opposite him and a waiter appeared from nowhere with a jug of coffee. She said it first, to get it over with. 'Looks like our day out is off, then.' She looked across at the display of food at the side of the big room and added brightly, to hide her disappointment, 'Shall we get something to eat?'

He shook his head. 'I never eat at this hour. You go.'

Why had he asked her to have breakfast with him, then? Hope twitched inside her. Maybe . . . She didn't let herself finish that thought, but turned resolutely towards the buffet. How people could start their day without a proper breakfast, she would never understand. She piled fresh fruit salad into a bowl and spooned creamy yoghurt over it for a starter.

He grimaced as she set it down. 'Rather you than me.'

'I'm always hungry in the morning.' She began to eat.

He said nothing until she had swallowed several spoonfuls, then asked idly, 'What are you doing in Northumberland anyway? We got interrupted when you were going to tell me last night.'

She stopped eating as a pang of grief shot through her and it was a moment before she could answer him. 'I lived near Alnwick till I was twelve. Then my parents were killed and I've never been back since.'

His voice was soft. 'So this is a sort of pilgrimage?'

'I suppose so.'

'What happened after they died?'

'My aunt and uncle brought me up. They live in Gloucestershire. They're like a second set of parents. They've been lovely to me.' And that was enough about her, she decided. 'Are your parents still alive?'

His expression became grim. 'My mother is. She's on her fourth husband now. My father died when I was twenty-three and I had to take over the business. It wasn't quite what I'd planned to do with my life, but if I hadn't, it'd have gone under. My father wasn't very attentive to the practicalities of business after my mother left us, you see.'

He stopped and looked at her in surprise. 'I don't usually tell people about that part of my life.'

'I'm honoured, then.' She was surprised at how different his face looked with that grim expression on it. Intimidating. Not a man to cross. 'I - um, think I'll get some bacon and stuff now.'

The grimness vanished and he gave an exaggerated shudder. 'Bacon at this hour? Ugh.'

She chuckled and went to fill her plate.

When she came back, he greeted her with, 'Why don't we go for a drive to Edinburgh instead of the walk? Even if it's raining, there are things to do in the city and if we take the coast road, the scenery is beautiful whatever the weather.'

He turned another of those devastating smiles on her. 'Unless you have any other preferences for our day out, Megan?'

'I'd love to go to Edinburgh. I've not been to Scotland since I was tiny. I've not been anywhere, really.'

'Do you dislike travel?'

'No. I've just never had the money. Or the courage to go anywhere alone. My parents were killed in a plane crash, you see, and they didn't have life insurance. If I hadn't been at a school camp, I'd have been with them.' That thought always made her shiver.

'That must have been hard for you,' he said softly.

Megan nodded. It had been very hard indeed and she'd taken over a year to settle down in Upper Shenstead. There hadn't even been anywhere private to weep in such a tiny cottage, where she had to share a bedroom with her cousin. And why she had told him about that, she couldn't think. She'd found long ago that people didn't want to hear about your personal griefs. But then, he'd confided something of his own past to her, so maybe he wouldn't mind.

His voice brought her attention back to the present. 'So we'll go to Edinburgh. And we'll call in at the garage that's repairing your car before we set off to arrange for it to be brought here, in case we're late back.'

His car was a Mercedes. It looked brand new and was very luxurious, silver with pale grey leather upholstery. She stared at it in dismay. He was definitely rich if he could afford to buy a car like this. Heavens, she was way out of her depth here. They moved in such different circles, it'd be stupid to hope for anything.

Hope? She wasn't hoping.

Was she?

Get real, Megan Ross! she ordered. Do not hope for the impossible.

He helped her into the car and all her good resolutions to remain cool with him flew away. Not that she needed helping, but she'd never realised how special it made you feel - cherished even - when a man fastened your seat belt for you.

They stopped at the garage and she asked what time she could pick up her car. Was it her imagination or with Ben beside her did the mechanic take it all more seriously?

'We close at three on Saturdays, but if it's just a blocked carburettor, I'll easily get it finished by then. No problem,' he said.

She tried not to show her disappointment as she looked at Ben. 'It won't be worth going as far as Edinburgh, then.'

'Nonsense.' He turned back to the mechanic. 'Can you take the car to the hotel? Give us an approximate price. OK. That sounds about right. You can swipe Miss Ross's credit card now and they'll get the signed copy for you at the hotel.'

'I don't think I can do that, sir. No offence, but I don't know anything about you.'

'Ring the hotel now and ask. Tell them it's for Ben Saunders.'

With a dubious glance at them, the mechanic disappeared into the office. He came out a few minutes later, falling over himself with eagerness to help them.

As they set off again, Megan asked in puzzlement, 'Why did your name work such magic? It was the same in the hotel. Am I supposed to recognise you?'

Ben shrugged. 'Of course not. I was involved in the sale of this chain of hotels a little while ago, so I'm known to the management, that's all.'

She glanced sideways at him. Real estate, he'd said, and she'd thought of selling houses. Selling a chain of hotels sounded like major league stuff to her. And he certainly didn't look like any salesman she'd ever seen. But she didn't like to pursue the matter. It'd sound as if she was nosing into his finances and she didn't want him to think she was mercenary. But it was great that he'd found a way round the problem with her car.

'I'm so glad we didn't have to give up our day out!' she said, beaming at him.

'So am I. I'm sure the weather will clear up later.' As if to give him the lie, rain suddenly pounded against the windscreen.

She chuckled. 'Oh, yes?'

'You wait and see,' he insisted.

There wasn't much traffic on the road and the rain made it feel as if they were in their own little world. She couldn't help glancing at him. Nice, dark hair, very well cut and gleaming as if newly washed. And she could smell a faint tang of after-shave, too.

She'd never seen the point in talking for talking's sake, so simply sat and enjoyed the scenery, which was beautiful even in the rain, commenting occasionally on a particularly lovely vista.

He seemed equally happy to travel peacefully.

'That's the coast road to Edinburgh,' he said as they came to a junction. 'How about we go that way? It's longer, but more picturesque than the inland route.'

'Sounds good to me.'

The road was beautiful. It twisted and turned along a mainly unspoiled coastline to reveal little bays with sandy beaches and villages with tiny fishing harbours, interspersed with jutting headlands. A ruined castle graced one of these, seen briefly in the distance during a break in the rain. Small islands lay in misty outline across the grey heaving seas.

'That's Lindisfarne.' Ben pointed. 'But it's high tide, so we can't drive across.'

'Really?' Holy Island, she thought dreamily. Saint Aidan building his monastery and converting the heathens of Northumbria. She'd read about it.

'Oh, stop!' she cried suddenly.

The car screeched to a halt. 'What's wrong?'

She could feel herself flushing. 'Sorry. There's nothing wrong. It was that.' She pointed to the castle towering on top of a cliff ahead of them. 'It's absolutely magnificent. What is it?'

'Bamburgh Castle.'

'It looks like something out of a medieval fairy tale. Could we stop and look round it, do you think?'

'Not if we're to reach Edinburgh in time for lunch.'

'Oh.' She couldn't hide her disappointment.

'But we could come back tomorrow morning. I don't have to leave until later in the day.'

'I'd love that!' She beamed up at the castle as they drove past.

'You look like a child promised a treat,' he teased.

'Well, it does seem a treat to me. The Cotswolds are full of quaint villages, but Northumberland is less tamed, somehow. And this coastline is magnificent. Why do I not remember it better?'

'Perhaps your parents didn't go out on day trips.'

'No. I don't think we did.'

'There's plenty of birdlife here, too,' he teased. 'Enough to suit you, I hope.'

'I'm not just into studying nature,' she protested. 'I love castles and history as well. Don't you think the architecture of today is graceless? Office buildings mostly look like piles of egg boxes to me!' She told him about her favourite stately home of all, the magnificently ornate Brighton Pavilion. He encouraged her to talk with the occasional question, sounding as if he was really interested. But after a while she realised how long she'd been talking. 'Sorry. I didn't mean to bore you.'

'You didn't. I enjoyed your enthusiasm. And you've made me want to go and see the Pavilion myself one day. I don't know why I never have. How about making a bargain? I'll show you Edinburgh. You show me the Pavilion.'

She tried to conceal her surprise. 'Oh. Well. All right. If you - you really want to.' She couldn't believe a man like him would make plans to see her again, but she would love to get to know him better.

'I do want to, Megan.'

The way he said her name made her breath catch in her throat and she couldn't think how to reply.

His voice was a low, amused purr from beside her. 'I'm afraid you're going to be disappointed in Bamburgh Castle, though.'

'Why?'

'Well, although it's basically medieval, it was the first English castle to succumb to gunpowder during the Wars of the Roses and most of it's a nineteenth-century reconstruction.'

'Oh!'

He chuckled. 'Confess it, you're disappointed.'

She couldn't help grinning back at him. 'Yes, I am rather.'

'Don't be. Bamburgh is still worth a visit, especially the King's Hall. There's some magnificent carving there, even though it's teak not English oak.'

His hand rested on hers for a moment, then he pulled it away and started up the car again.

It wasn't until they were approaching Edinburgh that she admitted to herself how very attracted she was to him. It was as simple - and as confusing as that. It wasn't just his looks, it was everything about him. He was so easy to spend time with.

But how did he feel about her? He wasn't just being polite if he'd talked about her showing him Brighton Pavilion. Surely not?

Could a man like him possibly be as attracted to her as she was to him?

She doubted it. He must have known a lot of women. In fact, they must have been falling over one another to attract his attention. So she'd better not let herself get carried away. Be sensible, she warned herself.

But oh, she didn't want to be sensible. She wanted to fly to the moon!

With him.

It was a relief to get out of the car in Edinburgh. They walked along the street side by side, not touching. She very aware of him, seeing the buildings they passed more as a frame for his face and lean body. His long, elegant fingers pointed and occasionally he caught hold of her hand to tug her across the road.

She had never in her whole life felt so bewildered by her own feelings. With other guys, she'd always got to know them gradually. Dating a stranger was - rather frightening, at least it was when you reacted so strongly to his lightest touch.

Edinburgh Castle was perched on top of a great mass of rock like a watchdog for the whole city and it was a relief to turn her attention to that. By the time they were inside, she was bubbling with questions and comments, thrilled by the castle's antiquity.

Once she caught him smiling at her. He was probably amused by her childish enthusiasm. Concentrate on the castle, Megan Ross, she silently ordered herself.

Only when they went into the War Memorial did she completely forget her own feelings, seeing the long lists of names inscribed there. 'So many men killed,' she murmured. 'Why do we have these wars?'

'For money. I'm rather interested in political history, actually. It's one of my hobbies.'

'I prefer social history. I like to find out how ordinary people used to live.' She added guiltily, 'I've spent a lot of my wages on books and my aunt's always complaining about the boxes stored in the roof space, my books and my parents' books too. I can't bear to throw any of them away.'

'Do you still live with your aunt and uncle?'

'No, I've got a room in my friend Sandy's house. She's pregnant and they're short of money, so it's a help for them, but,' she grimaced, 'one can grow rather tired of people talking about babies, especially babies not even born yet.'

He nodded, then looked at his watch and changed the subject. 'I don't know about you, but I'm getting hungry.'

'I'm not surprised. Don't you ever eat breakfast?'

He gave an exaggerated shudder.

She chuckled.

As Ben knew Edinburgh, she let him find them a restaurant. The minute they went inside, she felt overwhelmed by its plush décor and fussy service. There were no prices on the menu and nearly as many waiters as clients.

'Do you want me to choose for you?' he asked.

She pulled herself together at that. 'Good heavens, no!'

She decided on a starter of crudités, followed by veal in a cream and mushroom sauce. After that she turned with enthusiasm to the dessert trolley. Her plate was almost filled by a massive piece of the most delicious cheesecake she'd ever tasted.

When she had finished eating it, she looked up to find him staring at her.

'You're obviously not dieting, Megan.'

'I don't need to. I'm happy with the size I am.'

She thought he was criticising her until he said, 'That makes a refreshing change. I'm sick of paying a fortune for meals women only pick at. And I'm also tired of hearing about the latest diet craze from women who're skeletally thin already.'

That remark made him rise even higher in her estimation.

But the entente cordiale between them didn't last. She couldn't resist going into one of the souvenir shops because she knew how much her aunt loved little ornaments with place names on them.

'You're surely not going to buy that thing!' He took it out of her hand.

She snatched it back and glared at him. 'I most certainly am!'

'But it's ghastly!'

'My aunt will love it.'

'My aunt would throw it in the dustbin!'

Megan turned her back on him and, spine very erect, marched across to the counter and paid for the ornament. The cheek of him! Telling her what to buy. He might be gorgeous, but he was clearly arrogant as well. A good thing she'd realised what he was like. Now maybe she'd stop reacting so stupidly to him.

'Don't worry!' she tossed at him as they left the shop. 'Now the dreadful ornament is wrapped up, no one will know what I'm carrying, so you're quite safe walking next to me.'

He stiffened and stared at her. She stared right back. She wasn't having anyone criticising her family. They might not be rich or have very good taste, but she loved them dearly.

For the next half hour, as they strolled along the Royal Mile, they were scrupulously polite to one another. They took shelter from a brief shower, then, as they were about to cross a side road, Megan slipped and would have fallen but for Ben's quick reactions in catching her. She found herself pressed against a firm, warm body and her heart started to pound. 'Sorry. I'm not - not usually so clumsy.'

'The ground is quite slippery.'

When she tried to put weight on her left foot, however, she yelped and grabbed hold of him again.

'What's wrong?'

'My ankle. Could you just - wait a minute.' She moved her left foot experimentally and gasped as pain shot through it. 'Ouch!'

'Is it badly hurt?'

'Just twisted, I think.' She tried to make a joke of it. 'It only hurts if I move it.' What a clumsy idiot she was! Now what was she going to do? Her ankle was throbbing and she'd have to hop around like the Easter Bunny! That'd charm the socks off him.

'Then you'd better stop moving it, hadn't you?'

He made certain of that by scooping her up into his arms. She squeaked in panic and flung her arms round him.

'I won't drop you, Megan! Don't strangle me!'

They were almost nose to nose. 'I'm too heavy!' she breathed.

'Nonsense!'

'It's not nonsense. I'm five foot seven!'

'And I'm six foot two. What's more, Megan, I keep myself very fit. I promise faithfully not to drop you.' His eyes were warm with amusement.

'I feel such a fool,' she muttered.

'You're no fool, Megan.'

The skin of his face was beautiful, damp with rain but glowing with health and a golden tan that made him look so un-English. She had a most irrational urge to stroke his cheek.

Everything seemed to be happening in slow motion as he kissed her.

'I - ' she began, but he made a shushing noise, then gave her a long, curiously gentle kiss. When he drew away, she heard herself sigh in protest. She didn't want him to stop.

'You aren't wearing make-up,' he said huskily, his eyes seeming darker and full of mystery. 'You've no idea how attractive your skin is. I've been longing to touch it all morning.'

She closed her eyes for a moment then had to look at him again to make sure he really meant what he was saying. And his expression said he did, said he found her attractive. So she gave in and leaned her cheek against his shoulder. 'You're one hell of a kisser, Ben Saunders.'

'So are you. And I'd love to go on kissing you, but I must admit I can't carry you like this for much longer.' He stared round. 'Ah, there's a bench over there. Let's go and check out that ankle of yours.'

He put her down gently and Megan watched a passer-by, plump and middle-aged, stop to stare at Ben and sigh quite visibly for what she could never have.

'Now, let me look at your ankle.' He knelt down and very gently palpated it.

She couldn't help wincing.

'I agree, it's just strained. It'll hurt for a few days, but you don't need medical attention.'

She'd reached the same conclusion herself, because the pain was easing a little already. 'Thank you for coming to my rescue.'

'It was my pleasure. Look, I'll bring the car here. I shan't be long. Sure you'll be all right?'

'Of course.' She watched him stride off and sighed.

When he got back, he looked at her ankle and said, 'Perhaps we should go and get it X-rayed.'

She couldn't bear the thought of spoiling this wonderful day be spending several hours hanging around in Emergency. 'I'm sure it's only a sprain, Ben. I broke my arm once and it was quite different, a much sharper pain. Truly it was.'

'We'll see how it is when we get back to the hotel.' He helped her into the car, then produced a plastic bag and grinned at her. 'However, I did a first aid course once and they suggested this as an emergency treatment.' He opened it up, produced a big bag of frozen peas, then placed it on her ankle.

'Clever.' She adjusted it, then sat back to enjoy the return journey.

The tension gave way to a warmer feeling of companionship as he began to tell her of his other visits to Edinburgh and the things there were to do there - if she hadn't sprained her ankle. In return she told him about the Cotswolds, the small towns and villages she loved and some of the places tourists usually missed. After which she found herself talking about the protection of endangered species again, at his instigation.

'I've been too busy making money to play an active part in any projects like that,' he said, sounding genuinely regretful. 'But I have helped financially from time to time.'

'We need money as well as helpers,' she assured him.

'Do you chain yourself to trees?' he teased.

She shook her head quickly. 'I couldn't do that sort of thing. I'm more a behind the scenes helper. What I mostly do is observe, count the wildlife, deal with paperwork, that sort of thing. You need facts if you're to win support and anyway, I love watching how other creatures live.'

After a while they fell silent, and she leaned back with a sigh.

'Ankle hurting?' he asked softly.

'Not much.' As she looked round at the big silver car, the tall handsome man and remembered how it felt to be swept up in his arms, she couldn't help smiling.

He glanced sideways. 'What's so amusing?'

'Us.'

He looked puzzled.

She risked being honest. 'A luxury car and a handsome man. You've swept me off my feet - quite literally at one stage - it's like something out of a corny film.'

He flushed slightly. 'Merci du compliment.'

'De rien, monsieur.' Aha, she thought gleefully, that's thrown him off his stride, for once. 'You're the one who's blushing now,' she teased. 'You must know you're handsome.'

'I'm not used to being told so openly by a beautiful woman.' He concentrated on his driving.

He called me beautiful, she thought in wonderment. No one had ever called her beautiful before. But she felt beautiful when he said it. She watched the way his firm, well-kept hands moved on the steering wheel and unbidden came the thought of those same hands touching her.

'Penny for them,' he said quietly.

'Oh, I'm just enjoying the drive,' she said hastily.

By the time they got back, her foot was already feeling a bit better. As they stopped outside the front door of the hotel, he said, 'Wait a minute and I'll carry you inside.'

'I can limp along perfectly well if you'll just let me lean on you.'

'It'll be better for me to carry you.'

He bent down and surprised her by tilting up her chin to

kiss her again. She pushed ineffectually at him with one hand, not wanting to embrace in such a public place. But he ignored her and finished the kiss in a leisurely and eminently satisfactory manner.

She couldn't help sighing as his lips left hers.

When he bent towards her again, she gasped, 'D-don't!'

'Why not? You were enjoying it as much as I was.'

'I - you - we hardly know one another.'

'We will,' he said confidently.

He picked her up and she leaned against his chest, enjoying the sensation of being in his arms.

Then the spell was broken as a concierge rushed to fetch a chair. 'Shall I bring you a wheelchair, madam? Or a walking stick. We have quite a collection, left behind by guests.'

'A walking stick will be enough,' she insisted, feeling colour rise in her cheeks. 'I'm all right, really I am. It's just a sprain.'

When Ben had helped her up to her room he smiled. 'Dinner at seven?'

'I'd love to.'

'In my suite again? I'd come here, but I'm expecting a call from New York.'

'All right.'

'You'd better rest for a while. I'll get them to send up some ice, then I'll go and find out about your car.'

She'd forgotten that completely.

After another excellent dinner in his suite he looked at her across the table as she sipped a liqueur and tried to smother a yawn. 'You're tired and I have some international calls to make.'

She looked at him ruefully. 'There's something about a day in the fresh air, isn't there? I loved it, though.'

'Me too.'

He escorted her to her door again, watchful as she limped carefully along the corridor beside him using the walking stick. She didn't know what to say. Was this the end of their acquaintance or not? She'd been hoping he'd remember his promise to show her Bamburgh Castle, but he hadn't mentioned it again, so she hadn't either.

At the door she turned and gave him a determined smile.

He leaned against the wall, close enough for her pulse to start beating faster. 'Do you think your ankle will stand another outing tomorrow?'

She looked at him uncertainly. Did he really want to spend the day with her or did he just feel obliged to fulfil the promise he'd made?

He seemed to understand what she was thinking. 'I mean it.'

Delight flooded through her. 'My ankle will be fine.' And if it wasn't, she wouldn't tell him.

'Then I'll take you to see Bamburgh Castle, as promised. We may be able to hire a wheelchair to take you round it.'

How unromantic could you get? No way was she sitting in a wheelchair with her back to him. 'I'm sure I won't need that. My ankle's feeling better already. The ice did wonders.'

'I'll look forward to it, then.' He glanced at his watch. 'But I have to make those calls now.' He dropped a light kiss on the tip of her nose. 'Eight o'clock breakfast again?'

'Suits me. I'll meet you down there.'

Inside her room she raised one fist in a victory salute. He wouldn't be taking her out again if he wasn't enjoying her company.

Tomorrow, she thought as she drifted towards sleep, he's taking me to Bamburgh Castle. Tomorrow . . .

Chapter 3

The next morning Megan woke up filled with happy anticipation. She was going to spend another day with Ben, and if things went as she hoped - well, who knew what might come of it? Humming to herself she got up, then noticed the white envelope that had been pushed under her door.

Her heart sank as she picked it up. 'Megan' was scrawled across it in black ink. It had to be from him. He was only one person in the hotel who knew her. Why would he write to her, though, when they'd be seeing one another for breakfast?

Or would they?

She hesitated, then tore the letter open and scanned the few lines penned in a slashing, angular handwriting:

2 am

Sorry to do this to you, Megan, but I have to cancel our outing today. I've got to dash back to New York or the whole deal will come unstuck. I'm leaving in a few minutes.

I didn't want to wake you - you looked exhausted last night - but I've got your mobile number and I'll be in touch within a few days.

Look after that ankle.

Ben

Such bitter disappointment flooded through her that she couldn't move for a moment. The day lost all its colour and tears welled in her eyes as she hobbled back to slump down on the bed. She re-read the letter, but it was still the same sparse message. It didn't say any of the things she really wanted to know.

Like: was this just a tactful way to get rid of her? And if so, why? They'd been getting on so well. She'd been . . . hoping.

She went over the previous day in her mind and could see no reason for him to make excuses, none at all. He had seemed to enjoy her company as much as she'd enjoyed his. The New York trip must be genuine, then. He'd said he had calls to make when he left her.

If he'd had second thoughts about seeing her again, she wished he'd tell her straight out. This uncertainty was dreadful.

But he had made a point of taking her mobile number.

She couldn't be bothered with breakfast, just took her time about getting showered and dressed. It hardly mattered what she wore now, did it?

What was she going to do with the day? She pulled a chair over to the window and sat staring out across the gardens, her thoughts still in a turmoil.

She was a fool to be so disappointed! After all, she hardly knew Ben Saunders. And he'd certainly given her little reason to pin any hopes on seeing him again. She should just forget about him and get on with her life.

She didn't dive into relationships with people. It was one of her cardinal rules in life. She took her time, waiting till she knew them before allowing herself to care about them. She knew that put some people off, but that was how she had always been.

She froze for a moment as she realised that wasn't true. She'd only been like that since she'd lost her parents. Before, she'd been a happy, impulsive child. But when you knew how much you could lose, you were more wary of letting yourself care. It was only natural.

But with Ben things had felt different. None of those awkward silences she'd experienced with other men, no struggling for something to talk about. She felt as comfortable sitting quietly with him as she did when they were chatting. He was every woman's dream - not only attractive, but fun to be with, and kind, too. At least, he'd seemed kind.

She really shouldn't get her hopes up. He probably

wouldn't call.

When she noticed she was pleating the material of her skirt in her agitation, she smoothed it out again, wishing she could smooth out her tangled feelings as easily. She was sure she was attracted to him, very sure of that. But not at all sure of anything else.

She drew in a deep breath. She couldn't sit here all day mooning over Ben Saunders. She had her car back, thanks to him, so she'd check out of the hotel and visit the village where she'd grown up. After all, that was one of the reasons she'd come back to Northumberland. She wouldn't be able to do much walking, but she could park in the village and look round a bit. Face up to the memories of her parents and her childhood.

Good thing she had an automatic car and had hurt her left ankle. She'd have had trouble driving otherwise.

Welburn was the same old jumble of houses clustered round an untidy oblong of grass. There was a café in the house next to the general store now, and the latter was called a Minimart, with a bright red sign, but apart from that not much seemed to have changed.

The house she'd once lived in was on the opposite side of the green. It looked smaller than she remembered, but was larger than her aunt and uncle's cottage. Her father had worked in Alnwick; her mother had taught in the local primary school.

She smiled ruefully. She'd made the house into a palace in her thoughts and had thought of her life here as totally perfect. But it was just a smallish house, quite ordinary. And as an only child, she'd been lonely at times. Why hadn't she remembered that?

Her parents had travelled a lot. It had been a passion of theirs. Sometimes they'd taken her with them, mostly they'd left her with friends or with her aunt and uncle in the Cotswolds.

She'd had a reasonably happy childhood, but looking

back she realised suddenly how hampered such an adventurous pair must have felt with a child to look after, especially a child who was travel sick in cars and buses over even the shortest distance.

By the time they died, she'd just about grown out of that and they'd been planning a holiday in Australia for the following year, visiting a cousin of her father's. They'd told her about Australia, making it sound wonderful, and that had sparked an interest in the country that had never left her.

She didn't know why it had caught her imagination so strongly, but it had. It was stupid, really. She'd never even been across the Channel and here she was wanting to emigrate to Australia.

Sarah was right. In some ways she had got herself stuck in a rut. Well, that was going to stop right now. If she couldn't emigrate, then she'd find something else to do with her life. Be more proactive about it all. Running a group of offices in Upper Shenstead wasn't nearly enough. She had a little money saved and could afford to take a risk or two, move away, start a completely new life.

She should have come back here long ago and laid the ghosts to rest. She walked slowly across the road to look at her old home more closely and mentally said a proper farewell to it.

Now she was ready to move on.

She spent the rest of the day driving round, stopping occasionally to study the view or watch the world go by from the car. She felt at peace with herself and her ankle wasn't too bad, considering. She'd go home the next day and return to work on the Tuesday, as planned.

And Ben would ring her. He'd promised.

But even if he didn't, she'd still make some changes in her life.

By the time she got back to Sandy's, Megan wanted

only to lie on her bed with her ankle up. She had her mobile phone switched on and had half-expected to hear from Ben by now. Which was stupid really. If he'd had to rush back to New York in such a hurry, he'd be deep in business negotiations by now, or whatever he had to do there to make this deal go through.

What did she know about what a high-powered businessman did to make money?

Only - he should have been able to snatch a couple of minutes, at least, to call her. Shouldn't he?

Sandy greeted her with, 'I'm glad you came back early. I was feeling so fed up today!'

Megan could hardly walk away and ignore her friend's plea for company, so she smothered a sigh and sat down.

She had to explain why she was limping and mentioned her car breaking down. But she didn't mention Ben. Couldn't bear to expose such a fragile thing to public view.

When she'd finished talking, Sandy patted her belly fondly. 'It's really kicking hard now.'

Megan let her chatter on about the coming baby, then went to unpack and check the battery in her mobile phone. After lying on the bed for a while trying to read a book, she began to feel as if the walls were closing in on her. What she'd really like would be to go for a brisk walk, but that wasn't possible till her ankle got better.

In the end she decided to go and visit her aunt and uncle. They'd been complaining they hadn't seen enough of her lately.

As she was getting into the car her mobile rang. She stared down at it, almost afraid to answer the call, then growled in annoyance at herself and answered it. 'Megan Ross.'

'Hi, Megan. Ben here.'

'Hello.' Joy welled in her. He hadn't just been trying to get rid of her, then!

'I'm sorry I had to rush away like that.'

'Yes, it was a - a pity when we'd got another outing

planned and - ' She was starting to babble. She clamped her lips together.

'Megan, it looks like I'll be back in England on Friday. Can we meet then?'

'That'd be lovely.' She beamed at the mere thought.

'I'll try to ring you again during the week.'

'I'd like that.'

'Oh, hell, there's my taxi. I have to go now. Megan, I'm so glad we met.'

She sat staring at the phone for ages before she started the car, and couldn't stop beaming as she drove along. Well, why shouldn't she smile? He did want to see her again.

And she definitely wanted to see him.

As Megan limped up the path of her old home, she studied the neat little garden. Uncle John's great love, that garden. What else had he done with his life? Or Aunt Eileen? Raised a family and stayed here in Upper Shenstead where they had both been born.

And she'd almost fallen into the same trap, because it was a lovely village and felt so safe. Only - it hadn't been enough for her mother, who'd moved away from the area as soon as she left university, and it wasn't enough for Megan, she knew that now.

There had to be something more to life than counting birds in the local woods, however necessary that task was! She wanted a husband, children - and even some modest adventures. This weekend had shown her that much, at least, even if nothing else worked out.

She had to keep reminding herself of that, because Ben wasn't the usual sort of guy she went out with.

She knocked on the front door and called out a greeting as she opened it and walked straight into the front room. Uncle John, Auntie Eileen, Sarah, Don and little Amy were sitting with cups of tea in front of them, looking cosy and happy.

For a moment Megan felt like an outsider, then her uncle came across to hug her.

'Great to see you, Meggie-girl. You haven't called in for ages. You must have been working too hard.'

She returned his hug and the illusion of strangeness vanished.

'You look well,' her aunt said, sharp-eyed as ever. 'But you're limping.'

'I twisted my ankle. It's getting better.'

'You'd better keep it raised. John fetch her a stool. And that's a new sweater, isn't it?'

Her aunt never missed a detail. 'Yes. I bought myself a few new clothes. About time.'

'The colour suits you.' Sarah rocked the baby gently. 'How much did it cost?'

'Oh, too much. But I couldn't resist it.' She couldn't resist little Amy, either. She held out her arms and took the child on her lap for a cuddle. And couldn't help thinking yet again how much she would like a child of her own. A little boy with Ben's eyes and strong body, and -

What on earth was she thinking of? She hardly knew him.

She hid her blush by cuddling Amy. Well, she hoped she'd hidden it, but Sarah was staring at her sharply. Let her cousin stare. She wasn't going to tell Sarah anything about Ben. Two days wasn't long enough to get to know someone well enough to - to start making announcements.

And anyway, there was nothing to tell them about.

She smiled brightly at Sarah and looked at Don, who was sitting gazing at his little daughter with a fond smile. He was a quiet man, a good foil for lively Sarah, but Megan knew she could never marry a man like him. He was too placid for her, too focused on domesticity.

'You look as if you're plotting something, Megan,' her aunt said abruptly, just as she had when her niece was much younger.

'I am, I suppose. I'm - er - considering applying for another job somewhere abroad. France might be nice. Or Brussels.'

'You don't want to go working abroad,' said Don instantly. 'You've got a good, secure job here. Don't throw that away.'

Megan stared at him. He was a type England had been breeding for centuries, the sort of guy who went out to a foreign country and immediately set to work to make it into a replica of England. Now he really was a stick-in-the-mud.

'But I'd like to travel!' she insisted.

'You always said you were happy here,' Sarah protested.

Megan shrugged. 'I was. Now I'm not. I went back to Wellburn at the weekend and it sort of crystallised things for me. You were right about one thing. I have been stuck in a rut. But I'm about to climb out of it.'

'Bet you don't!'

'Bet I do.'

Sarah looked at her thoughtfully. 'I hope you do.'

Megan didn't stay long. Suddenly she felt greedy for life, for experience, for - Ben Saunders. You couldn't call it love, not when they'd only just met. But maybe, if she was lucky, love would grow from the attraction between them. She couldn't help hoping for that.

How long would it be before he called again?

Ben got back to his luxurious hotel room later than he'd expected. No use phoning her now. She'd be asleep. And the remaining days in New York were likely to be just busy as today had been.

How had he ever kept up such a frenetic schedule for all these years? He remembered the quiet peace of simply sitting with Megan in the car or strolling along a street, and marvelled at it. The time spent with her had been a golden interlude.

He ought to call Fran. He usually took her out when he

was in New York. She was good company. But she wasn't special. She had just helped fill the loneliness. She was lonely too and never stopped talking while they were together. And her hair was dyed red, not natural. Nor did it curl wildly and . . .

He frowned. What had got into him? He couldn't get Megan Ross out of his mind. He couldn't remember the last time a woman had affected him like this.

He frowned at the phone. Should he call her and wake her up?

No, better not. He got into bed, but it was a long time before he managed to sleep because he'd suddenly realised what he wanted to do. It was rash, it was risky, but he'd never wanted anything quite as much in his whole life.

He smiled in the darkness and began to relax. He'd taken a few risks in the past few years, but the one he was contemplating now outshadowed all the rest. Would Megan agree to it, though?

She had to. He'd do whatever was necessary to convince her.

Then he frowned again. Well, anything except lying to her. He wasn't going to start a relationship built on anything but the truth. Not with her.

On Tuesday Megan checked her mobile phone carefully when she got home, to make sure everything was working. But the battery was charged up and there were definitely no messages on her voice mail.

So he hadn't rung.

On Wednesday evening, the little red phone did ring and she picked it up with a pounding heart. But it wasn't him, just Sarah, trying to find out if something was going on. Megan didn't tell her cousin anything and refused an invitation to go and share a take-away meal with them on Saturday evening. Then she had to face a further grilling about what she was doing that night before she could get off the phone.

On Thursday, her personal phone didn't ring at all. She didn't know why she even bothered to have a mobile. She hardly ever used it, the stupid thing! She ought to get rid of it.

She found it hard to stay positive about Ben Saunders as the days passed without further word from him. He was still occupying centre stage in her dreams. Every single night. What was there about this man?

He'd said he'd see her on Friday, but hadn't made any arrangements. What was she supposed to do? Hang around until he deigned to call?

She'd just have to carry on as usual. What else could she do?

On Friday morning, the phone rang twice, once a wrong number and once a call from Mr Smethers, who was organising the protest vigil about a proposed development which would mean the end of a rather special wood, home to several rare plants. He wanted her to go out there on Saturday evening to replace poor old Mrs Branstone, who had 'flu.

'Sorry, but I've sprained my ankle.' Megan immediately felt horribly guilty because the ankle was almost better and she could perfectly well have taken part. After all, Ben hadn't even tried to ring her again, had he? She'd give him a day or two more, then she'd wipe him from her mind. Absolutely. Get on with her life.

On Friday afternoon, when she returned to work after doing the banking, she found Ben waiting for her in the foyer and stopped dead, not knowing what to say or do. For a moment, everything seemed to whirl around her, then a soft exclamation of surprise and pleasure escaped her control. 'Ben!'

He came across to kiss her cheek, which made the two receptionists nudge one another. 'Come up to my office,' Megan muttered, glancing meaningfully in their direction. 'It's too public here.'

He chuckled, but gave way to her insistent pull on his arm, thank goodness. She led the way briskly up the stairs.

Once they were inside her room he closed the door and leaned against it, watching her as she removed her coat. She hung it up slowly to give herself a minute's respite. She didn't know how to play this.

'I'm sorry I didn't call you again. There were a few glitches and I had to fly to Chicago as well in the end.'

She nodded and forced herself to look directly at him as she said what was in her heart, 'I wondered if you'd changed your mind about seeing me again.'

He smiled and shook his head. 'Definitely not.'

Her heart did a few quick somersaults and happiness began to flutter inside her.

'Of course I hadn't changed my mind!' he said. 'But the only times I was free, you'd have been asleep. I've had wall to wall meetings, thanks to a crisis.' He frowned. 'I should have rung, though, even if I'd woken you. I'm sorry.'

She nodded. She definitely wouldn't have minded being roused in the middle of the night by a call from him. She watched him stroll over to the window which had a glorious view of the rear of another building, a row of dustbins and a line of parked vehicles. Very romantic.

He turned to look at her. 'I'm really sorry I had to dash away from Northumberland without saying a proper goodbye. I was looking forward to showing you Bamburgh Castle.'

'Never mind. Another time, maybe.' She hoped she didn't sound as feeble-minded as she felt, but his nearness was having its usual effect on her.

He had crossed the few feet of floor and taken her into his arms before she realised his intentions. 'I'm glad you agreed to meet again, very glad indeed, Megan.'

The happiness expanded and warm tendrils of hope curled throughout her body.

'I love the way you blush.' His eyes were filled with

amusement.

'I'm always embarrassed by it.'

'Don't be. It's very attractive.'

The door banged open and a voice said, 'Oops! Sorry!'

Megan tried to move away, but Ben's arms remained firmly clasped around her.

The solicitor from the just down the corridor grinned at her from the doorway. 'Sorry to disturb you, Megan, my pet, but that damned coffee maker's not working again.'

'I'll - er - call the service firm.'

'Thanks.' He winked at her and closed the door.

She put her hands to her hot cheeks. 'Oh, heavens! It'll be all over the building in two minutes that I've been kissing a man in my office.'

'Who cares?' Ben teased his fingers through her hair, releasing it from the clip she always held it back with for work. 'I love curly hair, especially when it's red.'

'Auburn,' she corrected automatically as she made another half-hearted attempt to pull away.

'What time do you finish here, Megan?'

She looked at her in-tray, then gave way to temptation. 'I can finish now, if you like. Karen can call up about the coffee maker and lock up tonight.' Karen would love to take over her job completely.

As they walked outside together she was very conscious of the eyes following them and even more conscious of the man striding along next to her. What did he want to do tonight? There weren't many places to eat out round here.

He stopped beside his Mercedes and clicked the lock control.

She pointed across the car park to her own vehicle, which looked even older and more battered in the cruel light of the sun. 'I'll have to take my car home first.'

'I'll follow you. Then we'll discuss what to do.'

When they parked at Sandy's, he got out and leaned against his car, looking more like a movie star than a businessman. 'Have you got anything planned for this weekend?'

'Well - no.'

'Good. Go and pack a bag. You can show me Brighton Pavilion. And we can talk about our future.'

She stood glued to the spot. Our future? This was going too fast for her. She wasn't ready to fall into bed with him yet, however strong the attraction between them.

He stared at her with narrowed eyes, seeming to guess what she was thinking. 'We can have separate rooms, if that's what's worrying you.'

'It is. I don't . . . ' She couldn't think of a tactful way to say it, so said baldly, 'I'm not in the habit of sleeping with someone I've only just met.' Even someone whose lightest touch turned her bones to jelly.

His eyes gleamed wickedly. 'I'll give my solemn word not to ravish you, if that'll make you feel better.'

She could not help chuckling. 'Thank you, Sir Jasper!'

The gleam in his eyes became more pronounced as he added casually, 'Unless you change your mind, of course. I would never refuse a request from a lady.'

She stood very still, staring up at him. She had never believed that physical attraction could sweep you off your feet, but he had only to smile like that for her stomach to tie itself in knots. She tried for a more everyday tone, but wasn't sure she achieved it. 'Well - all right. Brighton it is. I'll go and pack. Give me fifteen minutes.'

She fled towards the house, away from the hypnotic effect of his body and those dark gleaming eyes.

But she couldn't resist turning at the door to smile at him and was delighted to see that he was watching her, smiling as well.

Inside she ran straight into Sandy, who screeched, 'Who is he?' and clutched her arm. 'Oh, wow, what a hunk! And just look at that car!'

'I met him in Northumberland.'

'And you didn't say a single word! You sly thing!'

Megan pushed Sandy gently aside. 'I have to pack.'

But of course her friend followed her up the stairs. 'What for? Where are you going?'

'None of your business. And look, do me a favour, will you?'

'Anything, as long as you'll introduce me to the hunk.'

'I'm not introducing you. Now will you do me the favour or not?'

Sandy sighed. 'You're mean and selfish and I'd do just the same if I were in your shoes. What's the favour?'

'Don't tell my family about him. It's too early.'

'Is it serious?'

'Could be.'

Suddenly Sandy hugged her. 'All right, Meggie love. I won't say a word.' She turned at the door to wink and add, 'Good luck!'

Outside, Ben watched Megan run into the house, admiring her long slim legs and flying hair. She was not only lovely, but transparently honest. And he loved her body, a real woman's body with soft curves, not a stick insect like the female lawyer he'd been dealing with in Chicago who had been brittle and defensive, always ready with sharp answers, always suspecting his meaning.

No, Megan was very special. And even thinking of her made him feel happy.

Memories of other women made him scowl suddenly. Because he was rich, some of them had expected expensive presents, utter luxury, wasteful extravagance that was against his nature. One in particular had been very difficult to deal with, so beautiful and apparently caring that it had been a while before he had realised how rapacious she was underneath that beautiful exterior.

He sighed, looked at his watch and began pacing up and down. Only ten minutes had passed. Funny. It seemed longer.

Did he dare he trust his instincts about Megan? He

shook his head in bewilderment. How could you ever tell for certain about another person?

The trouble was, he was booked to leave for Australia in just over a week and had intended to stay down under for a while. He could postpone the trip, though it'd be inconvenient, only he didn't want to. What he really wanted was to snatch Megan Ross up and carry her away with him. Cave man revisited.

A wry smile curved his lips. It was an unusual feeling for him.

He looked up to see her coming out of the house and pure happiness flooded through him as her face lit up at the sight of him. He took the suitcase from her and tossed it into the boot, then opened the car door, and flourished her a bow. 'Your chariot awaits, milady.'

She dropped him a curtsey. 'Oh, milord. I am vastly obliged to you.'

He threw back his head and laughed. It felt so good.

Chapter 4

When they arrived in Brighton, Megan watched in
amazement as the reception clerk fell over himself to
accommodate Ben's needs and the manager herself came
over for a word. There was an aura about this man, she
was beginning to realise. He had charisma, and it affected
everyone he met - not just her.

He'd booked a suite, of course, and this one consisted
of a spacious sitting room that separated two large double
bedrooms, each with its own bathroom. Megan felt
embarrassed when her battered suitcase was brought in
side by side with Ben's matching leather luggage.

'Choose whichever bedroom you like,' Ben said.

'They both look lovely.' She whisked her shabby case off
into the nearest bedroom, unpacking quickly so that she
could hide it in the wardrobe.

When she returned to the sitting room, his bedroom
door was open and she could hear him muttering to
himself inside. After a minute, he called, 'Can you lend me
some toothpaste, please, Megan? I've forgotten mine.'

She fetched her tube, feeling shy as she entered his
bedroom. 'Here you are.'

'Thanks.'

His fingers clasped hers for a moment and all the
oxygen vanished from the room. She drew in a deep
breath, trying to stay casual. She didn't fool him, of
course.

He grinned. 'Don't look so nervous. I've promised not
to ravish you.'

She managed to smile. Just.

He squeezed some toothpaste on to his brush and
turned on the tap. 'Why don't you wait for me in the
sitting room? I won't be a minute.'

When he rejoined her, he smelled of mint and freshly-
washed skin, seeming to glow with good health. He'd
changed into a casual shirt and slacks, with a leather

jacket, and his hair was ruffled, which made him seem younger and much more approachable. She liked him least in those dark business suits, she decided, elegant as they were. They seemed like armour, protecting the real him from the world.

'Well,' he said, smiling, 'are you ready for a hearty meal now? I know I am.'

He held out his arm and she linked hers in it. 'Where are we going?'

'To the restaurant here. I'm told it's a good one - and there's dancing.' His eyes gleamed at her in the subdued lighting of the lift. 'I like dancing with you.'

Except that the dance floor was about the size of a linen cupboard and the only way they could dance was to shuffle around pressed very closely against one another. Which soon had her feeling breathless again - and clearly was affecting him, too.

'It's too public a place for this sort of closeness,' he murmured in her ear. 'I can only take so much of it. Let's go back and try those desserts.'

But for once her appetite had vanished and she could only shake her head when the waiter brought the trolley across. She toyed with a cup of coffee while he ate quickly and neatly.

As he laid his spoon down, Ben began to yawn, caught her watching him and chuckled. 'My turn to fade early today. I ought to be wide awake, given the time differences, but I didn't get much sleep last night.'

'We can go to bed early if you like. It's no big deal.'

Another yawn caught him and he shook his head ruefully. 'I think I'll have to, if you don't mind. But I promise to be wide awake tomorrow.'

He held her at arm's length when they got inside their suite. 'I don't think I'd better kiss you goodnight in the way I'd like to. Not if I'm to keep my promise to refrain from ravishing you.' He grinned and brushed a very light kiss across the tip of her nose. 'Good night, Megan.'

She watched him go into his bedroom and it was a while before she realised she still hadn't moved away from the door. She hurried across to her own room.

Was she sorry or glad that he hadn't attempted to change her mind about them making love? She didn't know. But it took her a very long time to get to sleep, and her body wasn't feeling at all sensible. He was lying asleep only a few paces away and part of her wished she was with him.

But she had to tell him something before they got to that stage.

What on earth would he think of her?

The next morning, after a leisurely breakfast, they went out and walked round the Lanes together.

'Very picturesque,' he said, but he was looking at her not the shop windows.

'If you like jewellery shops,' she said lightly. 'Which I don't.' She noticed a look of surprise on his face. 'Why are you surprised at that?'

'Most of the women I know love shopping for jewellery, or clothes or make-up.'

'Not me.'

'What kind of shops do you like?'

'Bookshops. I can't walk past the door of one. But we're supposed to be going to the Pavilion today, aren't we? That'll be much more interesting than shopping.'

So they made their way there and she lost herself once again in the fascination of the Pavilion's interior, with its long, elegant galleries and beautiful furniture.

After a while, she asked, 'What do you think of my favourite stately home?'

'I think it's fascinating. Look at those chandeliers! Magnificent! It's like a fantasy world.'

On this visit she found herself looking at him more than the magnificent décor. She could just imagine him in regency costume, black tail-coat and stand-up collar, with neatly-tied cravat and knee-breeches. Shades of Mr Darcy and Pride and Prejudice!

He clipped one arm round her waist to pull her out of the way of two American tourists and she forgot about everything, but the warmth of his arm. 'Your eyes have gone all dreamy,' he murmured. 'What were you thinking about?'

'Oh, nothing much. Just – um, imagining a scene from one of Jane Austen's books.'

'I've not read them, but I enjoyed the TV series.'

She looked at him in surprise. 'You did?'

'Yes. Jane must have had a fine sense of the ridiculous.'

As they'd come to the end of the downstairs rooms, she suggested they sit down on the long bench at the back of the music room, something she always did. She loved this room. She didn't realise he was watching her with a half-smile on his lips until she turned to say something. The words died unspoken.

'No need to hurry,' he said gently. 'I'm enjoying it here, too. It must have looked magnificent in the old days, don't you think? Wouldn't you like to have seen it full of the nobility in silks and satins?'

'Yes.' Which showed they were in tune about some things, she thought. Well, they'd been in tune all morning. She couldn't remember when she'd last enjoyed herself so much.

Afterwards, they went up to the café and sat out on the terrace, looking down over the gardens. The sun was shining, making his dark hair gleam and she could sense that he too was feeling relaxed and happy.

Their eyes met and he gave her one of his devastating smiles. 'I love the way you don't fill every minute with idle chatter.'

'I'm useless with small talk,' she admitted. 'Never could get the hang of it.'

'That suits me fine. I've endured a surfeit of it over the years.'

For a moment his hand lay over hers, then he moved it away.

She felt like grabbing it, holding on to it. She didn't dare allow herself to do that. All she allowed herself was another half-smile at him.

In the afternoon they drove along the coast to Beachy Head because her ankle was aching now and of course he'd noticed. They sat in the car park looking out over the Channel.

'I've never crossed it,' she said, thinking aloud. 'You'd think in this day and age I'd at least have been to Paris, wouldn't you?'

'Why haven't you?'

'When I was a child I used to get travel sick. After my parents died, I was afraid of flying, afraid of going anywhere, really. Only Upper Shenstead seemed safe. Later Sarah and I went to work in London, but I was homesick for the country and she missed Don, so we came back after a few months. And since then, well, I haven't got round to travelling, somehow.'

After a thoughtful pause, she added, 'I don't really like living in cities.'

'I've had my fill of them, I must admit.'

'You must think I'm a fool,' she said abruptly. 'I've been nowhere, done nothing.'

'I've been nearly everywhere, but not for my own purposes usually, so I've done few of the things I wanted to when I was young. Most people seem to settle for a lot less in life than their youthful dreams, don't they?'

He didn't seem to be expecting an answer and sat staring into space for a long time, so she didn't interrupt him. Clearly he had his own demons to vanquish and like hers, his life seemed to be in a state of transition.

'If you could do anything you wanted, what would it be?' he asked suddenly.

'I'd like to travel a little.' She hesitated, because what

she was going to say might send him running for cover. 'Then I'd like to marry and have a family. I envy my Cousin Sarah her daughter and they're trying for another child now.' She waited for some scornful comment, but he surprised her again.

'I want a family, too. Unusual ambition for a man, isn't it?'

'If no one wanted a family, our species would die out. Is there some reason why you want one particularly?'

'Yes. Apart from it being a natural desire, there's a sad reason. A friend of mine died recently. He and his wife had put off starting a family for too long and he found he had cancer. The treatment meant he could no longer father a child. It made me realise I'd pushed my luck far enough. Which is why I'm selling my business and changing my life.'

He stared blindly across the gardens. 'I want to settle in Australia. I've bought a piece of land there and - '

She gasped, staring at him in shock. 'Australia? I don't believe it!'

'Why not? It's a great place to live.'

She tried to laugh but it came out bitter rather than amused. 'I know it is. I even applied to emigrate, but they turned me down. They don't need people with secretarial training, thank you very much. If I'd been a nurse or a computer whizz, it'd have been different.'

'Or if you'd been rich enough to buy a business. When I applied, they welcomed me with open arms on those grounds. It's amazing what money will do for you.'

His mouth had taken on a sneering twist, which gave him that intimidating air again. She frowned, not liking his tone. 'Don't knock money. I wouldn't have objected to having enough money for Australia to welcome me with open arms.'

'Were you very disappointed?'

She nodded. It still upset her to think of it. She'd put a huge amount of effort into checking out what life was like in Australia.

'I'm sorry.'

His voice was gentle and the warmth was back in his face. She forced a smile. 'Oh, well. You can't have everything you want in this life, can you?'

'Sometimes you can. Most of it, anyway. If you're prepared to take a few risks.'

She didn't bother to argue. A rich man's experience of the world was bound to be different to hers. And she had never been into risk-taking.

By the time they got back to the hotel, she was feeling footsore, though happy.

He drew her over to the couch. 'I'd like to talk to you about something, if you don't need to lie down or anything.'

'I'm not such a weakling.'

He sat down beside her, sitting slightly sideways, his eyes on her face. She was beginning to feel puzzled. What did he want to talk about that made him look so solemn?

'We've got on well today, haven't we?' he began.

She nodded.

'And there's no denying the fact that we strike sexual sparks off one another.'

'Well, um, yes.' She clearly hadn't been doing such a good job of hiding her reactions to him as she'd hoped.

He took a deep breath. 'So I wondered if you'd consider marrying me?'

She gaped at him. 'What?'

His expression was serious, his gaze not faltering. 'You heard me perfectly well.'

'But - it's too soon, surely, to talk of marriage?'

'I don't think so. I believe you and I would be able to build a good life together. We're not only physically attracted to one another, but we share several interests - and we both want to settle down and have a family. You even want to live in Australia.'

She stared down at her clasped hands, her mind in turmoil. He did mean it! And the trouble was, she was so attracted to him, she was tempted to say yes. Which would be a foolish thing to do on such a short acquaintance.

'Megan?' he prompted. 'Talk to me. Tell me what you're thinking.'

She raised her eyes slowly to meet his, frowning. 'I don't know what to say. I think it's you who should do the talking. I mean, we hardly know one another. Why rush into something as important as marriage? People usually live together for a while nowadays to see if they're compatible.'

He reached out to take one of her hands, raising it to his lips and then clasping it in both his own. 'I can't see any need to waste time. But this is more rapid than I would have chosen because I'm booked to go to Australia in a couple of weeks. I don't want to lose you.'

'But . . . we don't know one another properly. It's usual to fall in love before taking such a huge step.'

'Well, I don't intend to pretend this would be a love match. Actually, I don't believe in love at first sight or anything stupid like that. Our marriage would be for much sounder reasons.'

She pressed her lips together. He might not believe in love, but she did.

He stared blindly across the room. 'Marrying for sound reasons was the way they used to make marriages in the past, and I believe it's just as valid as today's madly-in-love matches, half of which are simply madly-in-lust. And half of which fail.'

He waited, as if expecting a response from her, but she couldn't think what to say. She definitely did believe in love.

His tone grew scornful. 'You've only to study the divorce rate, Megan, if you want proof that the current method of meeting life partners doesn't work particularly well. Divorce has never been higher. I've seen so many people I know marry, divorce, remarry, as if they're jumping on and off some sort of roundabout. I don't want that - that madness. Marriage is too important to be treated lightly.'

'Whatever your reasoning, it's still too soon for us, Ben. We really ought to spend more time together first before we take such a big step. Even live together, And later perhaps, if we continue to get on well . . . ' That was what she'd always planned to do, anyway. She couldn't dive into marriage with a stranger, a man she hardly knew.

'Unfortunately I have to go to Australia to fulfil the conditions of entry. I'd intended to stay there for a year or two. If we got married, if you could see past tradition, I think it would work brilliantly. It'd make a wonderful honeymoon trip, too, because I'm stopping off in Singapore on the way for a few days to tie up some more loose ends in my business.'

When she said nothing, he frowned and took her hand, pulling her closer. 'You have only to say you're not interested in me and we'll forget all about it. But I rather thought that we were getting on quite well.' A light kiss on her cheek made it hard for her to breathe steadily, let alone think clearly. 'Megan, I'd really like to marry you.'

She sagged against him, loving the feel of his arms around her, relieved when he didn't say anything else, just held her close, giving her time to think.

She was surprised how tempted she was to say yes, but no, that would be stupid. Hadn't she always vowed not to marry unless she could find someone to love as much as her parents had loved one another. Even as a child, she'd known how close they were. 'Couldn't you - come back to England for a visit now and then, Ben? We could spend more time together then and - and - '

'If you had a job here that you loved, and a life which fulfilled you, I'd consider doing that. But you don't. You're bored with your job, restless. Why, you'd even tried to emigrate to Australia! I'd probably come back in a few months and find you'd gone to work in Brussels or somewhere similar. If you want a change so much, why not make it with me?'

She stared at him, shaking her head slowly in disbelief. 'Do you always make such rapid decisions?'

'If it's necessary, yes. It's the way I tend to operate.' He frowned and started to jiggle some coins about in his pocket. 'I don't really want to come back to Europe again for a year or two. I've had my fill of jetlag and waking up in a different city each night.'

He began fiddling with a strand of her hair. 'I've been waiting a long time for my freedom, Megan. Five years ago I bought a house and some land, two hundred acres actually, in Western Australia.'

'Two hundred acres?'

'Yes. Fronting on to a lake.'

'It sounds gorgeous.'

'It is. Mainly untouched bush. You'd love it - the place is full of wildlife and I mean to keep it that way - well, most of it. Though I don't want you to marry me for the down under wildlife experience, but because we get on so well. Be honest and forget about tradition. What is there to prevent you from marrying me, Megan?'

Nothing! Except her own fears. She didn't say it aloud, but couldn't help thinking it. 'I couldn't just quit my job.' That sounded feeble even in her own ears.

'Your employers would understand the special circumstances.'

'Then there's my family.'

'We could go and see them tomorrow afternoon after we get back.'

'But I haven't said yes.'

'You haven't said no, either.'

Why hadn't she? she wondered. She looked at him. She'd never met a man she found so attractive. She'd enjoyed their time together enormously.

'It's a crazy thing to suggest,' she said hesitantly, then

thought what a pitiful argument that was.

'Then be crazy, for once,' he urged softly.

'Don't tempt me.'

He gathered her in his arms. 'I warn you now, I intend to do all I can to change your mind.'

His lips came down over hers and within minutes she was clinging to him and kissing him back with equal passion. But when she realised she was losing control, she pushed him away, breathing deeply.

He moved back, his eyes probing hers, his expression solemn. 'Marry me, Megan. I'm sure we could be happy together.'

'Could you - just go to bed now and leave me to think about it?'

'If that's what you really want.'

But she didn't know what she really wanted. She only knew she couldn't think with him holding her. 'Yes, I do.'

When he'd gone the room seemed empty and perversely she felt like rushing after him. But she didn't. Instead she walked slowly into her own bedroom and got ready for bed, taking refuge in her familiar routines.

What would life be like if she said yes? It could be - glorious, exciting.

What would life be like if she said no? If she let him go?

Dreadful! She couldn't bear the thought of it. A line from Hamlet jumped into her mind 'How weary, stale, flat and unprofitable seem to me all the uses of this world.' Trust the Bard to express it so vividly.

Her cousin's taunt came back to her. Was she the sort who'd remain in a quiet rut for the rest of her life? Wanting more, being given an opportunity for more, but not daring to risk reaching for it? She shivered, though not from cold, and wrapped her arms around herself. For the first time she began to seriously consider saying yes.

Marry a stranger! It was the craziest thing she'd ever heard of. Only he wasn't quite a stranger now. He was - Ben. Kind, intelligent, sexy, good-looking. Every girl's dream.

Whose dream would he become if she let him get away?

Oh, this was madness. Why was she even considering it?

Then the solution came to her. She'd offer to go out to Australia with him, live with him for a while, get to know him. Of course! Obvious.

Before she could have second thoughts, she flung open her bedroom door and went across to his. There was a light on inside, so she knocked. If there hadn't been a light, she'd have knocked anyway.

'Come in.'

She opened the door and took a deep breath. 'We don't need to marry. I can just come out to Australia and live with you for a while. That'll give us time to get to know one another.'

He looked at her, his gaze steady. 'I'd rather we got married and committed ourselves to one another. And it'll make everything so much easier. The Australian immigration people can be very fussy about issuing visas.'

'But we're - strangers.'

'You don't feel like a stranger to me, Megan. Do I really feel like one to you?'

She looked at him in exasperation. 'No. Well, not exactly. Look, I'm trying to be sensible here.'

'I'm not. I've spent too many years being sensible and responsible.' He leaned back against the pile of pillows, hands crossed behind his head. 'You're half way there, Megan. Why not go the other half? Why not take a risk and marry me?'

'I can't believe I'm hearing this.' She turned on her heel and marched out, slamming his door shut, then slamming her own as well. Of all the exasperating people! He was crazy. She should stick to her guns and refuse even to think of marrying him.

Only he was right . . . she was half-way there.

She went to stare at herself in the bathroom mirror and

saw a face where fear was the dominant emotion. She
didn't like that. She wasn't a coward - was she?

Going back into her room, she lay down on the bed and
pulled the covers up to her chin. No, that was too hot. She
tossed them off again. The pillow was hard. She punched
it a few times, but it stayed hard. And she stayed wide
awake.

After a few minutes she gave in and sat up. There was
no way she was going to get to sleep. No way in the world.
Switching on the light she looked for the book she usually
kept next to her bed, then remembered that she'd
forgotten to bring one in her hurry. She lay down again.

But the thought of marrying Ben wouldn't go away and
his words kept echoing round her brain. Why not take a
risk and marry me?

She crept into her bathroom again, trying not to let him
know she was still awake. When she looked into the
mirror, she didn't look scared this time, but she did look
apprehensive. Was that an improvement?

'Dare I?' she asked her reflection.

Why not? it seemed to reply.

She clapped one hand to her mouth. She was going
crazy.

But her blood was singing through her veins and she
felt more alive than she had done for years.

'Am I really thinking of accepting?' she asked herself
again as she crept back to her bed.

Yes, she was.

She didn't expect to get to sleep, but no sooner had she
made that decision than she began to relax. She woke to
find it daylight and herself lying in a tangle of bedcovers.

Someone knocked on the door. 'Megan, are you all
right? '

She blinked and sat up. 'Yes. Um, what time is it?'

'Nearly nine o'clock.'

'Heavens, it's not like me to oversleep. Give me half an

hour.'

'I'll get them to send breakfast up here. We haven't finished our talk yet.'

'You are stark raving mad, Megan Ross,' she told the tousle-headed idiot in the mirror.

The idiot smiled back at her. 'I know.'

She stepped into the shower, still smiling.

When she went out into the sitting room he was waiting for her. She looked at him and as he raised one eyebrow, she gave him a rueful smile and asked, 'Do you think craziness is infectious?'

His smile lit up the room. 'Does that mean you'll marry me?'

'Yes.' She yelped as he swept her off her feet and swung her round, then kissed her so hard the world continued to spin around them.

'You won't regret it,' he promised. 'We'll have a wonderful life.'

'I can't believe I'm doing this.'

'Trust me. It's right for us.'

She did trust him. But she still felt surprised at what she was doing, still questioned whether it was right.

Chapter 5

After a long, slow breakfast, Megan took a deep breath
and said, 'I'd like to discuss the practicalities.' She wasn't
going to be completely foolish about this.

He frowned. 'All right.'

She deliberately chose to sit in a chair rather than next
to him on the couch, because with his body touching hers
there was no way she could think straight. 'I - um, think
it's important to get our expectations of each other quite
clear. I want our marriage to last.'

His voice softened. 'So do I. Very well. You go first.
What do you expect of our marriage, Megan?'

She swallowed hard, trying to sound calm and
reasonable, when in reality she felt flustered and
uncertain. 'Well, I hope for a more interesting life than I
would have if I stay in Upper Shenstead. And - and
companionship. A family - later.'

'You're not expecting romance and roses? Because I
won't pretend about that. I simply don't believe in love at
first sight, let alone romantic love.'

His voice sounded clipped and his expression was
scornful. 'Of course not,' she said. 'We didn't exactly meet
and fall head over heels in love so you can't call this a
romance!'

She saw his expression relax a little. What did he have
against romance, for goodness' sake? 'But if you want to
buy me roses, I won't object.'

He nodded, but his suspicious expression softened only
slightly.

'I do know one thing, though,' she went on, for she had
a personal concern about what some men expected of
their wives. 'I don't want to be smothered in any
relationship! I watch Sandy, and all she lives for is Jim
and the baby. She's stopped having any opinions of her

own, because when she used to voice them, he would contradict her.'

Indignation rose in Megan. 'She actually lets him think for them both! And my cousin Sarah is nearly as bad. It's always "Don says – " and "Don thinks – ". So you should know in advance, Ben, that I'm not about to adopt your opinions wholesale or turn into a doormat.' Of that she was quite certain, if nothing else.

His expression softened still further. 'I would never expect you to parrot my views on life, Megan. In fact, I'd hate that.'

'What do you expect from a marriage, then?'

'A wife who'll be loyal to me, that above all.'

He was staring at her as if he needed to see her expression when she answered. She found that so surprising, she couldn't think what to answer.

As the seconds ticked past, he said harshly, 'You should realise that I won't countenance your having affairs with other men.'

Megan blinked in shock, then sat up straighter and glared at him. 'Do I seem the sort of person who would even want to do that?'

His face was sombre. 'You can't always tell. I don't think you are, but I still want to make it clear from the beginning that I'd leave you at once if anything like that happened. No second chances.'

'Well!' She didn't attempt to hide her indignation and tossed his own words back at him. 'And let me tell you, I'd leave you, too, if you were unfaithful to me. No second chances for you, either, Ben Saunders!'

He nodded and after a pause said quietly, 'Good. That's agreed. And I really want children. Two or three.'

'So do I.' Her indignation began to subside at that thought and she couldn't help smiling. 'And even if we haven't fallen madly in love, I hope we can become really good friends and - and learn to care about one another. It upsets me to hear you talk about being unfaithful before we're even married. It's the last thing we should be focusing on, as well as the last thing I'd ever do.'

His mouth twisted and his expression became hard again. 'Blame the people I've been associating with in recent years. 'Really rich people and celebrities aren't noted for their fidelity or their marital happiness, and I suppose that's made me cynical. And yet I've seen so many of them claim to be in love when they marry. That's why I insist on something different for myself, a relationship built on logic and honesty.'

She looked at him in surprise. Logic? When she sizzled at his touch. Melted into his kisses. Dreamed of him every night. When he had proposed marriage after they'd spent only three days together? That wasn't logic. It was sheer insanity.

She decided to change the subject. Let him think what they were doing was logical, if he could. She couldn't fault him on eagerness. 'What will our life be like in Australia?'

'Very different. I'm looking forward to a rest from the rat race - though there are still one or two bits of business I need to clear up. For you - well, it might be a bit difficult for you to fit in a career if we're living in the country. The Australian bush is very different from Upper Shenstead and the Cotswolds. The next house to where you live can be many miles away and country towns are mostly tiny places.'

'I don't necessarily need a career. But I do need something worthwhile to occupy myself with. Maybe I can get involved in conservation issues. The situation sounds to be as bad in Australia as here. And - and there are various other possibilities I'd like to explore. Creative options, perhaps.'

She didn't know him well enough to tell him about her secret ambition to write novels, or about the two short stories she'd had published in magazines during the past year – and been paid for, which made her feel like a professional writer. She hadn't told anyone about that, not even her aunt and uncle. The thought of becoming a novelist was too precious a dream. She couldn't bear anyone to treat it as if it was a hobby like embroidery.

She was working on her first novel now and it suddenly occurred to her that she'd probably have plenty of time to devote to it if she married Ben Saunders. A shiver of joy ran up and down her spine. This was all fitting together so well.

Only . . . it seemed too good to be true. How could this fairy tale possibly be happening to her?

He leaned forward slightly. 'All that remains now, Megan, is to arrange our marriage as quickly as possible. I'm sure my Aunt Louisa would do that for us, if you'd trust her. She lives in London and anything is possible there. We can just have a quiet wedding, if you don't mind. My aunt is the only member of my family whom I really care about and there are one or two old friends whom I'd like to invite. Would that be all right with you?'

'Won't she think it strange, you marrying someone you hardly know?'

'She's been telling me it's time I got married for ages. I think she'll be delighted, especially once she's met you.'

Elation sizzled through Megan, but it was followed by a jolt of pure terror as the marriage began to seem real.

He stood up and came to pull her to her feet. 'I shall be very proud of my beautiful wife.' First he raised her hand to his lips, which sent her wits scattering to the four winds, then he drew her into his embrace and began to kiss her. When he moved back, he was looking as stunned as she felt.

'No one's ever kissed me like you do,' she whispered.

'No one's ever roused me so quickly, either,' he admitted, his breathing deep and uneven. 'So it's agreed - we're getting married next week.'

Next week! How could he speak about it so calmly?

'Unless you're going to change your mind?'

She stared at him in silence, then shook her head.

Suddenly the thought of not marrying him, of going back to her humdrum life, was far more frightening than the thought of marrying him. 'No. I shan't do that.'

'Good. Because I don't want you to.' He waited a minute, then said, 'I suppose you'd better take me to meet your family. They won't want to see me for the first time at the wedding.'

'No!' It came out more sharply than she had intended and made him frown. Well, she didn't care. 'I'd rather present them with a fait accompli. I've already told them I was going to look for another job. I'll just - let them think I've found one.'

He looked at her in shock. 'You're intending to hide it from them?'

'Yes.' She realised she owed him an explanation. 'They'll try to stop me, I know they will.' And she might let them persuade her.

'I don't agree with that. They can't stop you unless you let them.'

'They raised me. I owe them so much. I'd find it hard to go against them.'

He shook his head in bafflement. 'This is the last thing I'd expected from you.'

'I mean it.'

He shrugged. 'Well, you know your own family best. But if you change your mind about that . . . '

'I shan't.' She tried to smile at him and failed.

His voice softened. 'We'll do what you want, then.'

As they were driving back, they stopped for lunch. As she was finishing her meal, she realised that she didn't know much about where they were going to live than that is was in Western Australia. Her research into emigrating had shown her that the state was about ten times larger than Britain, so she said, 'You haven't told me where exactly in Western Australia you live.'

'My land is a couple of hours' drive south of Perth, the

capital. In the south-west, near the wine-growing district, though mine isn't the sort you'd grow wine on.'

For a while he talked about Western Australia and it sounded like an absolute paradise. White beaches, a warm climate, no snow. Palm trees everywhere, parrots and tiny honey eaters flying about in suburban gardens.

She sighed ecstatically as she slowly stirred a second cup of coffee. 'I can't wait to see it.'

'Western Australia does have a few faults, you know. Days when the temperature's over a hundred degrees and you're too hot and sweaty to think straight, mosquitoes, isolation, heavy rain sometimes in winter. And Perth is a long way from everywhere. The nearest city, even in Australia, is two thousand miles away.'

'Goodness!' But she couldn't help smiling. 'After the thriving metropolis of Upper Shenstead, I don't know how I'll cope with that.'

'I think you're a country girl at heart.'

'I am.'

All too soon they arrived back at Sandy's. Megan didn't want to say goodbye to him.

He took hold of her hands. 'You know where I'm staying and you have my mobile number. I'll ring you every evening.'

'Yes.'

He hesitated. 'You won't change your mind about marrying me, will you?'

For once he looked hesitant and uncertain of himself and she found herself smiling reassuringly. 'No. We're both clearly mad, but at least we've gone crazy together.'

His kiss left her in no doubt of her feelings. She did want to marry him. Definitely. And his question had shown that he too was a little nervous about all this, under that confident exterior, which made her feel so much better about it all. She didn't want to marry a man who was always sure of himself. She wanted to marry the warm, friendly man with whom she had shared a few very precious days.

But although she felt happy and excited, she slept badly that night. Very badly. Ben Saunders seemed to have staked a claim to her dreams. His kisses made her melt with longing. What would his lovemaking be like?

She was so inexperienced, she was beginning to worry that she might disappoint him.

On the Monday, Megan gave in her notice and asked to be allowed to leave work that same day, explaining only that she had unexpectedly obtained a position in Australia and needed to take it up straight away.

After sitting through a hurriedly organised farewell party in the afternoon, she went back to tell Sandy the same story, though this time it was punctuated by shrieks and questions, especially when Sandy found out she was going to be working for the hunk with the Mercedes.

'Are you sleeping with him?'

'None of your business.'

'Megan Ross, you are so infuriating. Why will you never share your feelings and hopes like a normal woman? You keep everything to yourself.'

Megan blushed. 'I can't help it. I'm just - like that.'

Sandy gave her a big hug. 'Well, I love you anyway and I'm going to miss you horribly.'

On the Tuesday Megan went through her possessions, fending off more questions from Sandy as she tried to decide what to take with her. Resolutely she discarded most of her older stuff, all except the books, which could be packed and sent on once she was settled in Australia. She would take them over to her aunt and uncle's that evening, when she went to tell them her alleged news, and ask if they could be stored in the attic with her other boxes.

After lunch she rushed out to the shops to make a few purchases, including smarter suitcases. She intended to turn up in London looking like the fiancée of a successful international businessman, not like Cinderella come to town in her rags to marry a Prince.

She stopped to smile. Ben did seem like a fairy tale hero sometimes.

Tuesday evening was the most difficult time of all as she tried to explain to her aunt and uncle that she'd got a job in Australia and was leaving at the end of the week. She'd never lied to them before and felt weighed down with guilt, but somehow she didn't dare share her fragile dreams and hopes about herself and Ben with anyone. They might ridicule her or be horrified. And she couldn't bear that.

In the end her aunt and uncle sat in near silence, looking at her so unhappily her heart twisted with pity. 'It's not that I don't love you. It's just that I have to . . . to see something of the world and this . . . well, it's a golden opportunity.' But she could tell they were hurt and puzzled, and that took the edge off her excitement.

Sarah and Don were away in the Lake District, so she went home to write her cousin a letter that would explain about the alleged job. She had to write it three times. The first effort was so stilted it didn't sound like her. The second got spotted with tears. The third was short, promising a longer letter as soon as she was settled in Australia. It would have to do. Even to write that had torn her apart. Sarah was more like a sister and she would miss her far more than Sandy.

Megan had the feeling she was living in a dream, or in a world like one of those surreal Ascher drawings where you followed stairs round in circles that seemed to be going down and yet were leading you back up to your starting point. If Ben had been with her, she would have felt better about it all, but although he rang every evening, that wasn't the same. She needed to be held by him and see his smile.

Although she couldn't tell him that what she was doing

frightened her, it really did. In the darkness of the night she admitted that to herself, but at no time did she change her mind.

Just for once in her life she was going to take a risk and nothing, absolutely nothing was going to stop her from marrying Ben Saunders.

On the Wednesday, Sandy was going to drive her to the nearest station where she would take a train up to London to stay with Ben's Aunt Louisa. She was leaving the car with Sandy's husband, who had promised to sell it for her on commission and pay the money into her bank account.

It seemed a moment of supreme poignancy when Megan took the very last key off her key ring. She stood staring at the empty steel circle for a moment or two. Hardly anything left now of her old life. She fingered the worn leather tag which said A Present From Brighton. It had been bought for her by her aunt years ago, but it was ragged and dirty now and she'd been meaning to replace it for a while.

Should she keep it? No! She clicked her tongue in annoyance at her own sentimentality and threw the key ring into the rubbish bin.

A fresh start, she told herself firmly. That's what she needed.

Besides, Ben hated objects like that. They'd had their first and only near-quarrel about the ashtray she'd bought for her aunt.

Once she'd closed the last suitcase, she stood by the bedroom window for a long time, seeing nothing, lost in her thoughts. Australia was so far away! She would have no one to turn to there if things went wrong.

She made an angry growling noise in her throat. Nothing would go wrong. Of course it wouldn't. She wouldn't let it.

She picked up the suitcase and went downstairs. 'I'm ready.'

When Ben met her at the station, the world seemed to click into a clearer focus. He smiled at her and helped her with the luggage, stowing it in his shiny car, then opening the door for her. As they stood looking at one another, she felt suddenly shy.

'I'm glad you didn't change your mind,' he said softly.

'Were you worried I would?'

He nodded. 'Terrified. Stupid, isn't it? But I didn't want to lose you. I'm sure we're doing the right thing, you see. Quite sure.'

She nodded, pleased that he'd been worried too.

He smiled. 'Right, then, let's go and introduce you to my aunt.'

Louisa Griffen must have been about sixty, but she had a timeless elegance that made Megan feel very gauche and untidy when they first met. But the warmth of Louisa's welcome and her obvious fondness for her nephew soon broke the ice.

'Go back to work, Ben!' Louisa ordered, after she'd fed them lunch. 'Megan and I have a lot of things to work out.'

He grinned. 'Don't I have any say in the arrangements?'

'You've had your say. Now we have to see if Megan approves of what I've done so far. Besides, you said you had an appointment this afternoon.'

He glanced at his watch, exclaimed in shock and stood up.

Megan blinked in surprise as she watched him. It was as if he had changed personality entirely. The warmth had gone from his face, replaced by a cool expression that betrayed nothing of his thoughts.

'I'll be back this evening, as we arranged.'

She walked with him to the door, feeling shy again. He kissed her absent-mindedly on the cheek and was gone before she could say anything. Not that she had anything special to say, but she had expected a proper kiss at least. Disappointed she went back into the sitting room.

'It's very kind of you to let me stay with you and I'm really grateful for your help with the wedding arrangements,' she told her hostess.

Louisa smiled and waved one hand dismissively. 'Oh, I'm happy to do that. I've sorted most of it out already. It's not hard. The Royal Aztec is a first class hotel. I only had to go and talk to one of their function organisers and it was settled.'

'I should be paying for that,' Megan worried. 'It's usually up to the bride's family to deal with that side of the day.'

'My dear, Ben won't even notice the money. And I gather your family would. He said you'd not told them you were getting married. Is that wise? Have you changed your mind about that?'

'No.'

After a short silence, Louisa said, 'Well I hope you'll let me stand in for your aunt, then. We ought to discuss the wedding dress first, don't you think? I presume you don't want a traditional gown and veil?'

'Goodness, no. But I would like something pretty.'

'We'll go shopping together tomorrow. I know a rather special little boutique and there's a hat shop nearby. How about something romantic and Edwardian?'

'Have you been reading my mind?' Ben had been perfectly correct, she did like his aunt. Very much indeed.

Half an hour later, as they were finalising the menu for the small reception, Louisa laid one hand on Megan's and said, 'I'm glad my nephew's found the right woman at last. You'll be good for him.'

Megan blinked at her in surprise. 'Will I? Can you tell so quickly?'

'Oh, yes. I'm sure of it. You're so blessedly normal and practical. And you're not obsessed with your own body and appearance. In our circles there are some women who waste all their money and time on clothes and jewellery. I was terrified Ben would choose someone on appearances only. I'm already sure that you're more than just a pretty face.'

Megan grimaced. 'I've never been into jewellery and make-up. I'm an outdoor girl, really.' She chuckled. 'Though I am normal enough to enjoy flattering clothes and I do want to look special on Monday.'

'You will. We'll make sure of it. Welcome to the family, Megan.' She gave her a big hug.

Which made Megan feel even more guilty about not telling her own family what she was doing.

That evening Ben took her to the theatre, to a hit musical show which she'd once expressed a desire to see. She was touched that he'd remembered and couldn't believe he'd managed to get tickets at such a short notice. She enjoyed every second of the performance, but as they came out, she couldn't suppress a yawn and saw him smiling at her.

'It's been quite a week!' he said sympathetically.

'The most amazing week of my life.'

They stood still and people flowed around them like water. Neither spoke but they smiled and their hands were linked, and that was all they needed to feel good about life.

Eventually he tugged her forward again. 'I think I'd better get you back to my aunt's early. I have some figures to check tonight. One of the two people I'd kept on to help clear up the final details was suddenly offered a terrific job in Brussels. I couldn't hold her back, but it means everything is taking longer than I'd expected. Do you mind?'

'Not at all.'

'You're very undemanding,' he said wonderingly.

'What should I be asking for that I haven't got?' she asked. Besides, she still felt as if everything was slightly unreal, as if it couldn't possibly last.

On the Thursday, Megan had her first quarrel with Ben.

He came round for breakfast at his aunt's flat and when Megan opened the door to him, said without preamble, 'I worked late and got a lot more done than I'd expected so that I could take some time off today to buy you some new clothes.'

She stared at him in shock. 'But I've got plenty of clothes. I'll find something special for the wedding, of course - your aunt's going to take me to a boutique she knows - but you don't need to buy me anything.'

'Look, most of the things you wear are not . . . ' he paused then said bluntly, 'well, to be frank, they're not of good enough quality.'

'Oh. Well, I'll get one or two very smart things then. I do have some money of my own, you know!'

'I doubt it's enough for the sort of clothes I mean.'

'I don't want to take money from you before we're even married.' She could feel her hands clench into fists and her spine go rigid. She was not marrying him for his wealth!

'Look, Megan, the money's nothing.'

His tone was so impatient that annoyed her still further. As if her feelings didn't matter. As if she were a doll to be dressed before being brought out in company. She stopped trying for calm and let her anger show. 'No, but my independence matters a lot to me!'

'Don't be silly!'

She glared at him. 'And what's more, I don't intend to start married life by letting you order me around. You aren't buying an obedient doll for a wife!'

'I didn't think I was buying anything!'

Louisa came into the room, paused and would have backed out, but Ben turned and said through gritted teeth, 'Will you see if you can talk some sense into her, Aunt?'

'I will if you'll calm down too, Ben. What's wrong?'

'She won't . . . '

'I don't . . . '

'After you.' He waved one hand in a sarcastic flourish.

It was an effort for Megan to control her voice. 'He wants to play King Cophetua to my beggar maid, and I don't like it.'

Louisa raised her eyebrows questioningly at her nephew.

'She won't let me buy her some better clothes.'

'I'm sure you discussed it with her tactfully, Ben.'

He flushed. 'I told her the truth. We'll be mixing with people who buy from the top designers. I was actually trying to save her from embarrassment.'

Louisa gestured to the chairs. 'Do you think we might sit down to discuss this or do we have to remain standing?'

He flung himself into an armchair and Megan sat down on the very edge of the one opposite.

'You know he's right, Megan,' Louisa said gently.

'Well, he doesn't have to be right in that tone of voice!'

'He's never been famous for his tact.'

Megan breathed deeply.

Ben folded his arms and stared out of the window.

Since the older woman was still looking at her quizzically, Megan sighed. 'I suppose I'll have to let him.'

'Don't do me any favours!' snapped Ben. 'It's your clothes we're talking about.'

'You will feel a lot more comfortable if you have the right things to wear, dear,' Louisa coaxed. 'I was going to take you to some quite expensive places myself.'

'Do you want to come?'

'No. I think you can manage without me and I still have a few of Ben's friends to contact. We'll get your wedding outfit tomorrow.'

Ben opened his mouth. 'Look, I – '

'Keep quiet for the moment, Ben Saunders! I don't like your tone of voice, either. It's no wonder you've upset her.' She might have been talking to a naughty schoolboy.

Megan looked sideways at Ben and found that he was staring coldly at her down his long, finely chiselled nose.

She raised her chin and eyeballed him right back. 'I'm not marrying you for your money,' she said clearly and emphatically, 'so I don't like being the object of your charity!'

'Charity! What the hell do you mean 'charity?' You'll be my wife!' He ran one hand through his hair. 'What does the money matter, anyway? I just wanted you to feel comfortable.'

'The money does matter to me,' she said, wondering how to make him understand. 'I've never had much, you see.'

'I was poor enough, myself, at one stage, just after my father died. I do remember what it was like to have to count every penny.' For a moment his gaze was on his memories, then his eyes came back into focus and he smiled at her. 'Megan, I'm sorry if I sounded officious. It's just that I've only got today free and there's so much to do now Julie's left.'

She immediately felt guilty. 'I'm sorry, too. I - I'm just not used to the idea of you being rich yet. And I don't want you to think that I - '

'No one could ever think that you're a gold digger, Megan.'

'I'll go and get my coat, then.'

As she passed him, he caught her hand for a moment. 'I'm actually looking forward to buying you some pretty things.'

When he smiled like that, the last of her anger slipped away. Since she'd come to London she'd seen a different side of him, the serious businessman with a zillion calls on his time. That side made her feel nervous and alienated sometimes.

Get over it, she told herself. No one is perfect.

They had to visit the Australian authorities to deal with her visa. Because she'd been turned down before for a working visa, they had records of her personal details.

This time there was no question of turning her down, only of proving who she was and showing them the details of the medical she'd had early that morning.

'That was surprisingly easy,' she said as they left the building.

'I'm investing a decent sum of money in the country. That makes a big difference.'

His money again. The thought that he was rich made her feel uncomfortable sometimes. She didn't even know the details of his finances, and definitely wasn't going to ask.

'I need a coffee injection,' he said. 'Let's find a café. I think there's a good one nearby. What time are you meeting my aunt to look for your wedding outfit?'

'Not for another hour.'

'Good. We can have something to eat and rest a little. I don't know about you, but I've felt like a spinning top this week.'

'Me, too.'

They didn't chat much, just sat and relaxed together. But it felt good.

By the Friday afternoon, Megan was exhausted with so much shopping. She was thrilled with the wonderful outfit Louisa had helped her choose for the wedding and had pulled it out to admire it a few times.

Louisa was meeting some old friends for afternoon tea and had invited her along, but she'd refused. She was looking forward to staying home and spending a quiet hour on her own. She might even read a humorous romance novel she'd bought today.

When the phone rang, she sighed but went to pick it up.

'Mrs Griffen?' The caller didn't wait for an answer, just asked, 'I wonder - is Ben there?'

It was a woman's voice, husky and sounding rather sexy. The familiar way she drawled his name set Megan's hackles rising for no obvious reason.

'This is Mrs Griffen's flat, but I'm not Mrs Griffen,' she said, keeping her voice expressionless.

'Oh, I suppose you're the domestic.'

The scornful way the woman said that made Megan feel angry. On a sudden impulse, she said, 'Yes, madam.'

'Look, is your mistress there?'

'No, madam.'

'Well, when do you expect her?'

'I couldn't say, madam.' She heard the caller breathe deeply and mutter something that sounded like 'stupid idiot' and that made her feel even angrier.

'Look,' the impatient voice went on, 'perhaps you can help me instead. I saw Ben, Mrs Griffen's nephew - Ben Saunders, that is - in Oxford Street. His flat's been sold and his office closed down. I'm a close friend and I'm in London unexpectedly for a few days, so I wanted to get in touch with him. Surely his aunt knows where he is? Or perhaps he's staying with her? At the very least, you should be able to find me his phone number!'

'I don't think I can help you, madam.' Megan scowled at the phone. Who did this arrogant female think she was talking to in that patronising tone of voice?

Speaking even more slowly and loudly, as if to an idiot, the caller said, 'I've just explained that I'm a close friend of his. My name's Cynthia Berevic. You can at least tell me whether he's staying there!'

'I'll refer your query to Mrs Griffen. Do you wish to leave your number.' Megan jotted it down quickly. 'Is that all, madam?'

'No, it's not. I'll be telling Louisa how uncooperative you've been! You'll be lucky to keep your job!'

Megan grinned at the phone. 'Oh, I'm leaving at the end of the week, madam, so it's hardly worth your while complaining.'

The phone was slammed down at the other end.

Megan stared at it, her amusement fading. Who was Cynthia Berevic? She didn't like the idea of other women in Ben's life - and the way this one had spoken to her annoyed the hell out of her.

Two hours later Louisa came in, carrying a bunch of flowers and looking relaxed and happy.

'You had a caller,' Megan said, when they were settled in the sitting room chatting.

'Who?'

'Someone called Cynthia Berevic.'

Louisa stared at her in shock. 'What's she doing in London?'

Megan tried to appear casual. 'She didn't say. Who is she, exactly?'

'Someone Ben used to know. She married a friend of his about eighteen months ago. An Australian. Nick Berevic is also into property development, which is how he and Ben met.' She looked at Megan with a conspiratorial smile. 'The Berevics live in Sydney, on the other side of Australia, so you won't need to see much of her.'

'Was this woman a - well, a close friend of Ben's?'

'Used to be. More than a friend, obviously, but that's been over for a long time, thank goodness. I never did take to her. And Nick's a close friend of Ben's, too. He's a really nice man.'

Louisa chewed at one fingertip thoughtfully, then said slowly, 'I wonder what she wanted with Ben. She surely doesn't think that he would . . . ' She broke off and shrugged. 'What exactly did you tell her?'

Megan could feel herself flushing. 'I, um, pretended to be your maid and said I'd refer her query to my mistress. In the end she threatened to get me sacked for being so uncooperative.'

Louisa roared with laughter. 'Oh, I'd love to have heard that!'

Megan smiled reluctantly and her anger began to fade. 'She was absolutely furious.'

'Well, you just referred her question to me and I don't

think I'll sack you this time.'

After another thoughtful silence, Louisa said, 'Look, Megan, I think we should forget all about Cynthia's call. I shan't return it and there's no need to bother Ben about it. After all, their relationship is ancient history now. He won't want to invite her to the wedding, I'm sure.'

Megan nodded slowly.

'Well, I think I'll go and take a quick shower. What time is Ben picking you up tonight?'

'About seven.'

As Megan sat wondering why Louisa did not wish Ben to know that this woman had called, her mobile phone rang. His voice was abrupt. 'I'm afraid we need to have dinner with one of my former clients tonight. I'll pick you up around seven, as agreed, but you'll need to wear something extra smart. That blue thing we bought would be OK.' He put the phone down without waiting for her to reply.

Megan slammed the receiver down and breathed deeply. When Louisa came back, she asked, 'Has Ben always been so abrupt and - and arrogant? He just tosses orders at me and doesn't bother to ask whether it's convenient to do something. I've a good mind to refuse to go out to this dinner tonight!'

Louisa put an arm round her shoulders. 'He used to run a rather large company and it's inevitable that he's got into the habit of ruling the roost - especially when it's something connected with business. It'll take a while to train him out of it, I'm afraid, my dear. Is tonight worth making a fuss about this?'

'I suppose not.'

But as she got ready, Megan couldn't help worrying. Since she'd come up to London she'd hardly had any time alone with Ben and tonight would be no different. She could feel a distance building between them and could see no way to prevent it.

Of course he had to tie up all his business

arrangements, she did understand that. But surely he could have postponed their flight to Australia for a week or two? They really needed some time together to build their relationship. Why was he rushing her into marriage at this breakneck speed?

And then there was this Cynthia person. Did Ben still do business with her husband? Did he still think about her?

Was she the reason he had said he wanted no pretence of romance?

Chapter 6

At six o'clock on her wedding morning, Megan woke in a state of blind panic after tossing and turning for half the night. She simply couldn't do this!

Grabbing her dressing gown, she marched into the kitchen, knowing Louisa would be there because her hostess was an early riser.

Megan clutched the dressing gown round her with hands that trembled. 'I can't go through with it! I just can't!'

Louisa looked up from making a cup of tea and her smile of greeting turned swiftly to concern. 'My dear, you look absolutely dreadful!'

'Did you hear what I said? I can't marry your nephew.'

Not like this, anyway. If things had been different. Perhaps if they had fallen madly in love . . . and whatever he said, she did believe in romance and love. Only they hadn't. She must have been crazy to agree to his proposal. She sank onto a chair, burying her face in her hands and repeating the only thing of which she was sure that morning, 'I can't do it.'

An arm went round her shoulders and a voice said in her ear, 'Tell me what's upset you so much, dear.'

Megan surprised herself by bursting into tears and sagging against the older woman, of whom she had grown very fond in the short time they'd spent together. 'It's not that I don't like Ben.' She liked him too much for her own good. 'It's just that we don't know one another well enough and - '

At that moment the phone rang. 'Oh, dear! Excuse me a minute.' Louisa picked the receiver up, listened for a moment, then mouthed, 'It's the hotel's catering manager. Ben rang them last night. He wants a few changes made.'

'He never said anything to me!'

Just then someone knocked on the door of the flat.

After a few seconds the knocking was repeated, more

loudly this time. Louisa put one hand across the receiver. 'Would you mind answering that, dear?'

Megan stood up, grabbed a tissue to mop her eyes and made her way to the door. When she saw Ben standing outside she said, 'Oh, no!' before she could think.

He stepped into the hall, looking at her sharply, and as she tried to turn away he grabbed hold of her arm. 'Having second thoughts?'

She gulped. 'Yes.'

His grip tightened slightly. 'Why?'

'I just - I don't feel right about it all.' She sniffed and searched for another tissue.

He thrust a handkerchief into her groping hand, and put his arm round her shoulders. 'Come and tell me about it.' The caring tone made her sob aloud and feel quite overwhelmed with guilt. She didn't resist as he guided her to a couch in the sitting room and sat down next to her.

'Tell me what the matter is, Megan! Is it me? Something I've done?'

'No, of course it isn't!'

'Then what is it?'

She tried hard to stop crying. 'I'm sorry, Ben. I just - it's not you, it's me. I can't go through with this. My family will be so hurt. And - and we're going so far away, so I won't even see then to explain.'

'Shh, now. Let's talk about it quietly.' He brushed a strand of hair from her wet cheek with his free hand.

The arm round her shoulders felt so warm and strong she leaned against him, sighing wearily. For a moment neither spoke, then she said accusingly, 'And what's more, you're not supposed to see the bride until the ceremony. It's bad luck.'

'Hey!' He held her at arm's length for a moment with a wry smile. 'How can you not be going through with it one minute and then worry about me seeing you before the ceremony the next?'

His index finger traced a line down her cheek, 'Such

beautiful skin,' he said softly then bent forward and started to kiss her.

Although she stiffened and tried to push him away, he simply captured her hands and continued to kiss her. As usual, his touch sent fire flaming along her nerves and made her forget everything else.

When the kiss ended, he said fiercely, 'We are most definitely going to get married today, Megan Ross. Things will work out all right for us. We'll make them work out. Trust me.'

She looked up into his strong face. Not only had no man ever made her feel like this before, and with the other men she'd dated, she'd often been glad when the fumbling had stopped.

He pressed one further lingering kiss on her lips. 'I think we have the basis for a very happy life partnership, Megan, and if you try to wriggle out of marrying me, I shall kidnap you and spirit you away to a gloomy castle where I shall force you to submit to my wicked lusts until you beg for mercy.'

She swallowed hard. 'I don't think that would take long. I - Ben, I didn't know it could be like that, just with a kiss!'

'It isn't always.' Even for him this desire that flared between them was something very special, a hunger dancing through him, but with tenderness twisting through the need.

You didn't ride roughshod over a woman like Megan. He'd guess she was quite inexperienced, that she'd only had one or two lovers, and that they hadn't really roused her. But there was passion beneath the freshness and honesty. And the thought of awakening it was the biggest turn-on he had ever experienced in his whole life.

But now wasn't the time for that. Now he needed to reassure her, make her realise that he really did want their marriage to be a success. Not for some reason as nebulous as being in love but because . . . He hesitated, finding it hard to put his feelings into words and in the end had to be satisfied with telling himself it was because they were so well suited.

He sighed and leaned back, her head cradled against his shoulder, not saying anything. It was another of the joys of being with her that you didn't have to fill each moment with meaningless chatter.

He saw her try to smile, then her lips quivered again.

'What is it?' he asked softly. 'There's still something wrong, isn't there? It's not me. Tell me what it is.' And he would fix it. Whatever it was.

She stared at him, feeling enormously reassured by the tenderness on his face. 'It's what you said in Brighton, Ben. You were absolutely right. It's this hole in the corner stuff with my family. I w-wish we had invited my aunt and uncle to the wedding.' Tears spilled down her cheeks. 'They've been like parents to me. I just - I can't hurt them like this.'

She could see the relief in his face even before he said, 'Is that all? I was afraid you'd taken a dislike to me.' He kissed the tip of her nose. 'The problem of your family is quite easily remedied. The wedding's not until two. Ring them up now and invite them.'

'But they - I - how? Ben, my uncle and aunt don't even have a car.'

'That's easy too. I'll arrange for a car to bring them up to London and I'll book a room for them in our hotel. They can even come and wave us off at the airport tomorrow. Will that make you feel properly launched into a life with me?'

Things were so easy when you had plenty of money, she thought.

When she didn't answer immediately, he asked again, 'Will it make you feel better if they come? Or is there something else worrying you?'

'Not worrying. I can't ask my cousin Sarah because she's away on holiday, but she'll be upset. But I have to have my aunt and uncle there at least.' After a moment's hesitation, she asked, 'Ben, am I being silly?'

His voice was cool and crisp now, where it had been soft and tender a few moments before. 'No, it's perfectly normal to want your family with you on your wedding day.'

He pointed to the phone. 'Ring your aunt and uncle now!' He started to stand up. 'I'll leave you some privacy.'

She listened and could hear a voice speaking in the kitchen. 'Your aunt is still on the phone. I can hear her. I'll have to wait until she's finished.'

'Use my mobile, then.' He took it out and flipped it open.

She grabbed his arm. 'Stay with me. Please, Ben! And show me how this fancy gadget works.'

She dialled the number with fingers that trembled and when her uncle answered, she couldn't, for a moment, speak. Then she managed to say in a quivery voice, 'Uncle John?'

'Megan, love! Is something wrong?'

'N-no. Everything's fine. Only - well, I'm getting married today and - and I want you and Aunt Eileen to come to the wedding.'

There was a splutter, followed by an incredulous, 'What did you say?'

Ben raised one eyebrow quizzically at Megan as the word was followed by a dead silence.

'Uncle John? Are you still there?'

There was the sound of a throat being cleared, then, 'Megan, did you say you were getting married today?'

'Yes.' Ben's arm went round her in a gesture of support and suddenly the final doubts fell away. She was doing the right thing and she was definitely going to marry Ben Saunders today.

'Who's the man?'

'He's called Ben. I met him that weekend I went to Edinburgh.'

'But - I thought you were going to work in Australia.'

'That was, umm, with Ben. He's going to live there.'

'Oh. Well, I don't know what to say, I really don't. You've taken me by surprise.'

'I want you and Aunt Eileen to come to the wedding, Uncle John. I know it's short notice, but please . . . '

He interrupted her. 'Megan-girl, are you in some sort of trouble? Because if so, you know there's always a home for you here. Or if it's money, we have some saved and . . . '

She smiled and looked apologetically at Ben, who could hear every word. 'No, I'm not in trouble, Uncle John. I've just - when I met Ben we - it didn't take us long to decide that we wanted to get married.'

'I can't take this in. Look, speak to your aunt, will you.'

There was a smothered murmur of voices, then her aunt's sharp tones on the phone, demanding to know if this was true, and if so, how had it all happened so quickly and why hadn't they been told about it before?

Megan tried again to explain, growing more incoherent by the minute with tears threatening again.

In the end, Ben plucked the phone out of her hand. 'Mrs Ross, Megan is a bit overwrought. May I introduce myself? I'm Ben Saunders, the man who's going to marry your niece today.'

'Oh, are you? Well, then, perhaps you can tell me why our Megan is so upset?'

'It's my fault. I've rushed her into it. The thing is, I have to fly out to Australia tomorrow and I can't get back to the UK for a while. So it made sense for us to get married now and for her to come with me.'

'Oh?'

He smiled. She sounded totally unconvinced and unimpressed, too. He liked that. 'Look, will you and your husband please come to the wedding, Mrs Ross? We'll explain things properly then. I'd love to meet you and I'm sure you'll want to meet me. Your being with us means a lot to Megan. She'll be really upset if you don't come.'

There was a moment's silence, then Megan heard her

aunt say briskly, 'Well, of course we'll come!'

'What about her Cousin Sarah?'

'She and Don are visiting friends in the Lake District this week.'

'There won't be time for them to get here, then, but I'll send a car to pick up you and your husband.' He handed the phone back to Megan.

When she put it down, she flung herself into his arms and hugged him ruthlessly. 'Thank you!' She smacked a kiss on each of his cheeks, and wiped her eyes determinedly. 'I must look a real mess! I'm sorry, Ben. I'm not usually such a fool.'

He eyed her up and down. 'Well, I have seen you looking better, I must confess. But not to worry, I've always had a weakness for women with red eyes and matching noses.'

She threw a cushion at him before asking the question that had been floating at the edge of her mind. 'What are you doing here at this hour of the morning, anyway?'

He grinned and gave a huge stretch. 'I'm on my way back to the hotel. I've been working through the night, tying up loose ends. Nothing's gone smoothly this week. I decided to drop in here on the way back and check that you were all right. You seemed a bit - strained last night.'

'I felt strained.' She laid her hand on his arm. 'Thank you for being so understanding.'

He put his hands on either side of her face and kissed her gently on each cheek in turn. 'My pleasure.'

She felt shy suddenly, so quietly tender was that gesture after the recent passion. 'I must go and wash my face.' She hesitated, then couldn't resist planting another quick kiss on his cheek.

'Give me your aunt and uncle's address first.'

When she'd gone, he stood staring after her and touched his cheek. It had been a simple child's kiss, but none the less sweet. He couldn't remember any other woman kissing him quite like that since he was a lad. He cleared his throat, but the butterfly impression of her lips was still quivering on his skin.

And he was still feeling roused, needful. It had been a long time since he'd had a relationship with anyone, let alone a continuing need that hummed within him all day long. His lips curved into a twisted smile. And none of the women he had wanted before had been at all like Megan.

He wasn't sure what that meant. All he was sure of was that he wanted to marry her and would let nothing and no one stop him.

Louisa was just putting the phone down as her guest entered the kitchen. 'Some people can't use one word when ten can be found. Who was that at the door?'

'Ben. He's still here - has a phone call to make.' Megan went across to fill the kettle.

'What's he doing here at this hour of the morning?' Louisa looked searchingly at Megan's tear-stained face. 'And is everything all right between you now?'

'Yes. I'm really glad he came. I was upset that my aunt and uncle weren't coming to the wedding, so we've just rung up and invited them. Oh, and Ben's staying for breakfast. He says he's been working all night. He's ravenously hungry.'

'Will you get some croissants out of the freezer and there's some ham in the fridge? I just need to check something with him.'

Ben looked up as his aunt entered the sitting-room. 'Hi.' He closed down his phone and put it in his pocket.

'What brought you round here at this hour? You're not usually an early morning person!'

He grimaced. 'I haven't been to bed, actually.' He lowered his voice and asked quickly, 'I wanted to ask you whether Cynthia has rung. She's in London, on one of her mammoth shopping trips. When she found I'd moved out of the flat, she rang the old office number and left a message on the voice mail.'

He grimaced at the memory of the provocative message she'd left with no thought about who might hear it, an entirely inappropriate message, considering they hadn't been together for over two years. And even if he had been free, she was now married to a good friend of his. He didn't cheat on anyone.

Cynthia clearly did. Well, he knew that already, didn't he?

He grimaced at his aunt. 'She ought to be looking after Nick, not shopping in London. It seems he had a heart attack a few weeks ago, luckily only a mild one.'

Louisa made a clicking sound of exasperation. 'I'll never understand what you saw in the woman. Or what Nick saw in her, either.'

'She's very attractive physically. Fools you for a while, till you realise she has no heart. Did she try to contact you?'

'Yes. She phoned here.'

He frowned. 'What did you say to her?'

'It was Megan who answered.'

'Oh, hell!'

'That girl can take care of herself. Don't underestimate her!' Louisa chuckled. 'Apparently she pretended to be the maid and was so uncooperative that Cynthia threatened to complain about her to me and get her sacked.'

He threw back his head and laughed, but the smile soon faded. 'I only hope Cynthia doesn't find out about the wedding. I wouldn't put it past her to turn up uninvited.'

'I thought she was safely married to Mr Money-bags!'

'If I read the situation rightly, since Nick's heart attack, he's not able to satisfy milady any more.' There was a touch of embarrassment on his face as he added, 'I don't really want to talk about her.'

'Me neither. You'll do far better with Megan.'

'Yes. I agree. I'm getting quite fond of her already.'

'That's quite an admission, coming from you.'

He shrugged, but couldn't help smiling at the thought of Megan's freshness and honesty - and the way she responded to him. He drew in a deep, calming breath and added mentally, And the way he responded to her!

'I've never been as sure of anything on a personal level as I am of marrying Megan.'

She patted his cheek, giving him a misty smile.

Just before noon, a black limousine deposited Auntie Eileen and Uncle John at the block of flats. They hovered awkwardly in the hallway of Louisa's home with the air of two people bearding a lion in its den.

When Megan rushed to kiss them, her uncle enfolded her in his arms, then held her at arm's length and scrutinised her face very carefully. 'You're going to make a beautiful bride, Meggie-girl. I wish my brother could be here to see you.'

'I do, too.' She had been thinking of her parents as she finished packing her things, studying a photograph of them and wondering if they'd have approved of Ben.

Her aunt's scrutiny was no less thorough. 'You look tired.'

'I didn't sleep well, worrying about not inviting you.'

She led them into the sitting room and introduced them to Ben, who had returned a few minutes previously. He was already dressed for the wedding in a light grey suit, with a white silk shirt and a tie in subtle shades of grey and pink that was a work of art in its own right.

Auntie Eileen's and Uncle John's expressions were still suspicious, but Ben was at his most charming as he introduced them to his aunt and urged them to sit down. In fact, Megan thought in annoyance, he was positively oozing charm. Could he turn it on so easily, then? Had he been merely pretending with her? Surely not?

After a cup of tea and some stilted small talk, Auntie Eileen said abruptly, 'I don't want to upset anyone, but we'd like to speak to our niece in private.'

Megan threw an apologetic glance at Ben and led the way into the dining room, where a light buffet lunch was set out. To her surprise, it was Uncle John who spoke first.

'What's all this about, Meggie-girl? How come you're marrying this stranger?'

'Don't you like him?' she parried, uncertain whether she could lie to her uncle.

'I don't know him. I'd never even heard of him before this morning, had I?'

She blushed and shame filled her. 'That was my fault. He wanted to come and meet you a couple of weeks ago.'

'Why didn't you bring him to see us, then?' Her aunt didn't look best pleased. 'Were you ashamed of us?'

'No, of course not!' She rushed across and hugged them both again to prove it. 'I don't know why, really. I just felt that you might try to stop me marrying him, and I didn't want to be stopped.'

Her Uncle John put his arm round her. 'So what changed your mind today, love?'

'I suddenly realised I couldn't get married without you two there - and Ben was so understanding, we rang you straight away.'

Aunt Eileen sniffed disapprovingly. 'Our Sarah's going to be furious she's missed it and I still don't see why there's all this rush.'

'Because he's got to go back to Australia tomorrow.'

'Australia!' Her aunt's voice lost all its sharpness and she blew her nose, before saying sadly, 'It's so far away, love.'

Her uncle patted his wife on the shoulder. 'Well, Eileen, as long as the girl's happy, that's all we should care about.'

'I've always wanted to go there. I did try to emigrate once, if you remember,' Megan reminded them.

'I was delighted when they turned you down,' Uncle John said flatly.

Standing in the doorway, listening to them, Ben

frowned. He hadn't considered that aspect before, but Megan was getting something she'd been denied by marrying him - permission to settle in Australia. He couldn't help wondering how big a part that had played in her decision to marry him.

No, what was he thinking of? She was the least scheming female he's ever met. He stepped forward, clearing his throat. 'I'm sorry to disturb you, but we need to eat lunch and then get ready.'

'All right, then, Mr Saunders. We've had our say.'

'His name's Ben,' Megan reminded them.

Aunt Eileen nodded, but didn't repeat his name, just studied him thoughtfully.

Later, as she was helping Megan change into her wedding outfit, she said abruptly, 'It looks as if you've done very well for yourself, my girl.'

Megan flushed. 'Ben's not short of money, if that's what you mean. But I'm not marrying him for his money.'

'Why, then?'

She sought for a simple explanation that would sound convincing and could only manage, 'Because he's gorgeous.'

'He is, rather.' Aunt Eileen gave a quick glance at her own reflection in the mirror, then turned to scrutinise her niece. 'That's a beautiful dress.'

They both looked at the reflection in the mirror. The slim, shapely young woman in ivory silk seemed a stranger to Megan. She couldn't possibly look so attractive. The slender, ankle-skimming dress fitted her perfectly and with it she wore a large picture hat, with silk flowers around the brim. Hints of an Edwardian lady in the style, and yet it was totally in today's fashion as well.

'Yes, you certainly look the part of a rich man's wife,' her aunt repeated. 'All My Fair Lady-ish. Now, let's go and get you married.'

She hesitated, then pulled Megan's face down towards

her and gave her a kiss, a thing she rarely did. 'And remember what your uncle said - there's always a home with us if things don't work out. And money for the fare back, as well, if you need it.'

'I have enough money for that myself. Thank you for caring, though.'

But Megan couldn't imagine needing to use her money to fly back to England. Ben's behaviour today had settled all her worries - well, most of them. She wasn't stupid enough to think their marriage would be all roses and moonlight. There were bound to be difficulties as they learned each other's ways and settled down. But a man who could be so kind and understanding would surely continue to make the necessary efforts to adjust to life together. As would she.

In fact, it would be a pleasure most of the time, she was sure.

Hope filled her, and joy, too. As they went outside to the limousine, the world seemed full of sunshine and light. This was her wedding day - and her groom was utterly gorgeous.

It was all going to work out for the best, she was quite sure of that.

After the wedding, which was held in a registry office with only the immediate family group and a friend of Ben's present, they went to the hotel to rest before the evening party.

The brief ceremony had seemed very unreal to Megan. Did those few sentences spoken by a smiling stranger really turn her into Mrs Saunders? She didn't feel very married yet.

She stared down at the ring they'd chosen. It hadn't been difficult to find something pretty when money was no object, though Ben had been surprised when she chose a very simple engagement ring and insisted on him having a wedding ring, too. He was wearing it now. She glanced down at his hand, then at her own.

'The rings look good, don't they?' he said as they sat together in the chauffeur-driven limousine. 'I'm glad you insisted on my having one as well.'

They exchanged smiles and she reached out to hold his hand, sorry the hotel was so close. She could have driven like this for a long time.

Once they got there, they were enveloped in fuss which made everyone in the lobby stare at them.

He chuckled. 'In the limelight again, Mrs Saunders.'

'Yes.'

'You shouldn't look so beautiful.'

She felt beautiful in this dress, but she still couldn't cope easily with the stares and attention. Sarah would have revelled in it, but Megan felt embarrassed by it.

She found the bridal suite at the hotel overwhelming in its sheer opulence. It was furnished with what looked like antiques, with paintings on the walls that must have cost a fortune. Two huge vases of flowers stood on small tables. What had those flowers cost? In fact - what was this suite costing? The thought made her feel uncomfortable.

When the concierge had gone, she and Ben explored the suite and she had to resist the urge to tiptoe around as if she had no right to be here.

'No separate bedrooms any more, thank goodness. If you knew how hard it was in Brighton to get to sleep with you so close,' he murmured with a wicked grin as he threw back the door of the bedroom.

She stopped dead in the doorway, gaping at the gigantic bed, with its drifting lace curtain suspended from a circular crown of gilded wood on the wall above. 'It looks like Sleeping Beauty's bedroom,' she said without thinking, then jumped in shock as his arms came round her from behind.

'Well, you're certainly very beautiful, but I don't intend us to do much sleeping tonight,' he murmured in her ear. 'And you're going to have to get used to me touching you from now on, Mrs Saunders. Or are you still nervous?'

She tried to relax in his arms, but couldn't. 'I'm sorry. I am a bit nervous. It's been a wearing day and there's still the evening to get through. You'd better tell me exactly who's coming.'

'I don't think you'd remember. I'd better confess now that I've invited more people than I had originally intended to join us in our celebrations tonight. Some business acquaintances, the rest of my relatives and a few people I knew at university.'

Dismay took her voice away for a moment, then she said faintly, 'I thought it was just going to be your close family and one or two old friends.'

'It was, until I realised how that would look. It'd look bad if I didn't do something to mark the occasion, and I didn't want to give anyone cause for gossiping about you, or our sudden marriage. Do you mind?'

'No, of course not.' But she did mind. She was rather nervous of entering his world of affluence, had hoped to postpone it for a while.

A big yawn suddenly prevented him from speaking. 'Look, it's not romantic, but would you mind if I took a short nap? I'm getting too old to go without sleep.' He looked at her shrewdly. He wasn't too old to want to take her to bed this minute, but he knew without being told that she'd be grossly embarrassed to make love, then go down and socialise. He was, he thought, learning to understand her. As much as one person ever understood another.

'Thirty-three isn't old,' she protested.

'It feels old at the moment.' He started to remove his trousers, yawning again.

'I think I'll slip out of this dress and put on a dressing gown.' If you could call that froth of black lace Louisa had bought for her as a wedding present a dressing gown. 'I'll sit in the other room and have a read while you sleep.'

She changed hurriedly, made nervous by the bare

muscular legs padding around the bedroom, but he made no attempt to touch her.

As he removed his shirt, Ben paused for another gigantic yawn.

He seemed to be tanned all over, Megan thought, staring in fascination at his broad shoulders and chest. She moistened her lips with her tongue and almost went across to him. He even raised one eyebrow as if inviting her.

No. She took a step backwards. Not now. Not with the evening's reception still to come. She didn't want one hair out of place as she faced these strangers.

She went into the living area and curled up on a white leather sofa with one of the glossy magazines provided by the hotel open on her lap. But didn't read a word or even notice the pictures. The scent of perfect pink roses filled her nostrils and her own reflection stared back at her from several gilt-framed mirrors.

Black lace negligée, red hair flaming above it, white sofa - and a terrified expression on her face.

You're being utterly stupid today, she told that reflection. What's got into you, Megan Ross? Snap out of it.

But she was not Megan Ross now. She was Megan Saunders. And somehow, she didn't seem to know herself any more. It had all happened too fast.

It wasn't that she was regretting the marriage, definitely not, but she felt as if she were being dragged along by runaway horses, galloping out of control, and who knew where she'd end up?

She took a deep breath. She'd end up happily married if it was up to her.

Only . . . that was up to Ben, too.

Chapter 7

Ben woke an hour and a half later as if he'd had an alarm clock next to the bed. He looked refreshed and suggested they get ready and go down early. 'I want to drink your health before the guests arrive, Mrs Saunders. Here, let me do up that hook.'

His hands on the nape of her neck made her shiver in anticipation. 'You make an excellent lady's maid,' she said, her voice coming out breathless.

'I'm going to be even better at helping you out of those clothes later on,' he murmured suggestively, his fingers toying with a lock of her hair.

'I wish there were no reception,' she admitted. 'I'd prefer it to be just the two of us.' And she would love him to help her out of her clothes - slowly.

He stepped away with obvious reluctance, offered her his arm and led her over to the mirror.

The immaculately dressed couple staring back at them both seemed like strangers to Megan. Was that really her? She had never looked so good, she knew. But it didn't seem like her. Didn't feel like her, either. 'You look very handsome,' she said quietly.

'And no man could want a more beautiful bride than you,' he said, then glanced at his watch. 'Better give your aunt and uncle a quick ring and suggest they join us downstairs as soon as they're ready.'

They went down to a function room on the mezzanine floor, where several attentive staff were standing around and a buffet table was half-prepared. A waiter brought them some champagne and when Ben raised his glass to her in salute, she clinked hers against it.

Then her aunt and uncle turned up, together with his aunt, and their few moments of peace and togetherness were over. The first arrivals followed soon after, then a stream of people.

Megan stood beside her new husband to receive their

guests' congratulations. They're only people, she told herself, but it didn't help because they were such confident, well-dressed people - and they all seemed to know one another.

She watched her aunt and uncle surreptitiously to make sure they were all right and was surprised at how relaxed they looked. Well, her uncle didn't get fussed about much and from the gleam in her eyes, Auntie Eileen was thoroughly enjoying this brief taste of high life and would boast about it to her many friends after they got home again.

Cocktails and intricate finger food were followed by a buffet meal of considerable opulence, and the rich people turned out to be just as greedy as anyone else, Megan noted. Had she not been so nervous, she might have been amused by it all, but she could feel the eyes on her and for once, her appetite had quite deserted her.

By the time the meal was over, her head was aching fiercely from lack of sleep the previous night and people's voices seemed to be alternately fading and booming around her. She sat through three brief but witty speeches, which taught her that her husband was both liked and respected as a businessman and colleague.

But people didn't say much about him on a personal level. No jokes about his quirks or times when things had gone wrong. Was that because they didn't know his other side?

Did she know it? she wondered. He was intelligent, charming and certainly good-looking, but she had little idea what was going on in his mind. Why had he pushed her so quickly into this marriage? She had thought that question answered, but today these people had made her wonder about it all over again.

Why would such a successful, confident man want to marry an ordinary person like her? Any one of these immaculately turned out women would have made a better partner for him in this world of wealth and style.

Ben leaned closer and murmured in her ear, 'Like animals at feeding time, aren't they?' which made her feel slightly better.

Another time he sighed and whispered, 'This one coming in now is the biggest bore in all London – no, all England.' But none of that feeling showed when he was talking to the man in question. Which made Megan wonder again whether she would know if Ben were telling her the truth or not. She hoped she would. Oh, if only this evening would end! She was exhausted!

Then a woman behind them asked another whether Cynthia knew about this marriage and Ben stiffened. As he swung round and glared at the speaker, the woman took a step backwards and hastily changed the subject.

Megan took a sip of wine, trying hard not to feel jealous, but she couldn't help wondering what this Cynthia was like. She wasn't going to ask about her, though. Certainly not! Besides, they'd probably never meet if the Berevics lived in Sydney. And Louisa said the affair had been brief and was long over.

The last guests started to take their leave. Megan shook their hands, feeling quite numb with fatigue. Her aunt and uncle had gone yawning up to their room half an hour previously and Louisa Griffen had followed shortly afterwards.

A parting suggestion from one man made Ben's smile go glassy and Megan blush.

'Sorry about that,' Ben said. 'Tim's a fool. '

Around them the waiters started clearing up in earnest.

Ben smiled. 'I'm exhausted! And you look as if you've been awake for three nights. But I think it went well. We've done our duty and now we can think of ourselves.'

'I don't know how you can stay alert with so little sleep.'

He put his arm round her. 'Its anticipation that's keeping me awake. Come on, wife! Time to retire to my lair. I mean to have my wicked way with you at last.'

She tried to smile, wishing she could recapture the

passion of their embrace that morning. Was it only that morning? It seemed like aeons ago.

In their suite she took a quick shower and put on the brand-new black lace nightdress that went with the negligée, a nightdress far more provocative than anything she would have chosen herself. She smoothed it out in front of the bathroom mirror, feeling suddenly shy of appearing before him like this, then took a deep breath and went back into the bedroom.

Ben whistled appreciatively and on his way into the bathroom stopped to run a fingertip across the tops of her breasts. 'Beautiful! This might just be the shortest shower on record, Mrs Saunders.'

She got into bed and lay waiting for him, her stomach churning and her throat dry. She wasn't sure he'd appreciate her inexperience as a lover. After a few seconds, she closed her eyes because the lights were hurting them.

Ben came out of the bathroom humming softly, then stopped as he saw how still the figure in the bed was. He walked quietly across and stared down at her. She looked young and defenceless, with utter exhaustion written all over her face.

'Pity,' he murmured, with a wry smile, 'but it'd be a shame to wake her.'

And he felt pretty tired himself, now he came to think of it. He climbed in next to her, expecting to have difficulty in getting to sleep in such an aroused state but, like his wife, he was overcome almost at once by sheer fatigue.

Worried that there was no sign of the newly-weds, Louisa phoned through and woke them at nine o'clock the following morning.

Megan jerked awake and realised in horror that she had fallen asleep on him on their wedding night. 'Ben, I'm so sorry! You should have woken me.'

He shrugged. 'The pleasure is only postponed,' he said softly, cradling one of her breasts briefly in the gentle warmth of his hand and planting a slow kiss on her lips.

'If it were anything else but a plane waiting for us, I'd tell it to go to hell,' he growled in her ear. 'But the airlines wait for no man. Come along, Mrs Saunders, your chariot awaits.' He turned at the bathroom door to grin and admit, 'And I fell asleep within seconds, too.'

Which made her feel much better. She hardly recognised him with tousled hair and a face flushed with sleep, but she liked the way he looked now. This was the man she had married, not the suave public figure of the previous evening.

And she, too, regretted that waiting plane.

What magic was this that he could touch her and she would melt? Surely, surely, an attraction this strong must lead to more than just a calm friendship? You're a fool, she told her reflection in the mirror. Don't ask for more than he can give, at least not yet. Impatience will only lead to unhappiness.

Auntie Eileen filled the drive to Heathrow with praise of the hotel and the food served the previous evening.

Uncle John was very quiet. Just as the newlyweds were about to go through Customs, however, he stopped Ben. 'Don't leave it too long before you come back to visit, lad.' He clasped the hand he had just shaken in both his. 'We'd like to get to know you better and we shall miss our girl. And don't forget your promise to look after her.'

Megan gave her uncle a final kiss and hurried through the waiting barriers with tears in her eyes, not even daring to look back or she'd have sobbed aloud. Ben's hand on her shoulder made her glance sideways. He wiped a tear off her cheek with one fingertip. 'I like the way you care about your family,' he said quietly. 'We'll pay their fares out for a visit and we'll go back to see them.'

She looked at him uncertainly, then someone behind them said 'excuse me' and they had to move on. But the concern for her in Ben's eyes comforted her, as did the promise to pay for her family to come out and see her.

Maybe she was worrying about nothing. Maybe things were really quite straightforward, and friendship and sexual attraction would be enough to start off a successful marriage.

And kindness. That never went amiss, either. Warmed by his understanding she settled down in her seat.

Singapore's Changi Airport was massive, so full of people and noise that Megan, who felt groggy from dozing on the plane, kept tight hold of Ben's arm as they made their way along in a buffeting crowd of tired travellers, all eager to get to their hotels.

They passed through Customs so rapidly she couldn't believe it. 'I thought they checked everyone for drugs,' she whispered.

'Only suspicious persons. And no one,' he added with a grin, 'would ever think you suspicious. Now, I'm expecting to be met.' His eyes searched the crowd and a man materialised, wearing a driver's peaked hat.

'Mr Saunders? I have your car waiting.'

They were driven to another luxury hotel. Just like the one in London, it enclosed them immediately in a warm cocoon of fuss. It could have been the one in London.

A young man took their luggage away even before they had finished registering and a beautiful Asian woman ushered them quickly across the foyer and into a lift which zoomed upwards to what Ben called the executive floors. Their guide opened the door to their suite and left them with a graceful inclination of her head.

Megan moved quickly from bedroom to sitting room, exclaiming in delight at the view. When she went into the bathroom she called out excitedly, 'There's a spa bath. Oh, Ben, I've never tried one before.'

Turning, she saw him standing watching her with an indulgent smile and looked at him uncertainly, suddenly worried that she was making a fool of herself. 'I must seem very naïve to you sometimes.'

He walked across to plonk a friendly kiss on her cheek. 'I like it. I'm sick of blasé people who never seem to enjoy anything except other people's discomfiture.'

He might like it, but she felt a bit embarrassed.

They moved by unspoken consent to stand by the windows. 'So many boats,' said Megan wonderingly, 'and all full of people going about their business.'

'We'll go for a trip round the harbour if there's time. How would you fancy a ride in a junk?'

'Could we? Oh, Ben, you make me feel like Cinderella at the ball!'

'Well, I'm no Prince Charming, I'm afraid.'

She eyed him sideways. 'You look the part - tall, dark and handsome - but . . . '

He looked at her suspiciously as she paused. 'Well, go on. Finish it! What comes after the but . . . '

'But just a trifle grumpy at times.' She pretended to shrink away from his mock anger.

'You'll pay for that later, woman!' He tilted her chin up. 'In the meantime, I'll take a small deposit on account.'

The kiss began gently and it went on until her whole body was bound up in it, till she was pressed tightly against every masculine inch of him. When he moved away from her, she had to clutch him or she would have gone spinning onto the floor.

He chuckled softly. 'No one ever kissed you properly before, did they, Cinders?'

'No.' She smiled at him. 'I think I'm going to need a lot of practice to get it right.'

He sighed and looked at his watch. 'I hate to say this, but I have a meeting to attend.'

'Now?' She could not believe her own ears. He was going straight to a business meeting on their honeymoon!

'I'm afraid so. I'd planned this trip before we even met. I couldn't have cancelled things without giving serious offence to some people whose goodwill is important in the finalising of this part of a multiple deal.'

She pulled away from him, trying to speak cheerfully. 'OK, then. You're forgiven.' But she knew she wasn't concealing her feelings very successfully.

'I really am sorry.' He looked at his watch again. 'Do you want to go out shopping or will you wait for me here? You only have to ring if you want room service. The hotel staff are very helpful.' He reached out to tease a strand of her hair into a curl, something he seemed to enjoy doing.

He sighed and let the curl drop back, then went into the bedroom, where he changed hurriedly into a clean shirt and dark suit. As he left, the kiss he planted on her cheek was distinctly absent-minded, his thoughts already elsewhere. 'I expect I'll only be a couple of hours.'

She swallowed hard and took a step backwards, away from the temptation to cling to him and beg him to stay. She had never considered herself the clinging type, but she kept getting an urge to drape herself all over him. 'I'll wait inside the hotel, I think. I'm a bit bewildered by all the crowds outside. When I've unpacked, I'll go down to that nice café off the foyer for a snack.'

'You can have something sent up here. Or eat in the executive hospitality area on this floor.'

'Oh, no! Much nicer to go down and watch people. It's one of my favourite pastimes.' She stopped in the middle of the room as it occurred to her that she had perhaps spent too much time watching other people in the past and not enough time living her own life to the full.

Well, she was going to enjoy life from now on. Every second of it. And enjoy her new husband, too. She was looking forward to tonight. If his kisses could affect her so strongly, what would his lovemaking be like? A delicious shiver ran through her at the thought.

Ben got back two and a half hours later to find Megan still sitting in the café in deep conversation with an elderly woman who looked like a retired schoolteacher. As she saw him, Megan made her excuses and walked towards him, beaming a welcome.

'How lovely! I didn't expect you back so soon.' Now, perhaps they could go out and start exploring. It was infuriating to have come to a romantic foreign city and then just sit around in a hotel waiting.

'Unfortunately I have to have dinner with the same people and their wives aren't coming.'

She knew her disappointment was showing clearly in her face. When had she ever been able to conceal her feelings? Swallowing hard, she managed a shrug. 'Well, if you have to - '

'It's a dreadful thing to do to someone on their honeymoon.' His tone was coaxing. 'Will you ever forgive me?'

With an effort she summoned up a smile. 'I can't enjoy the fruits of your labour and then complain when you have to work, can I? But I'll have to change some of my money or I'll not be able to do anything while you're away.'

He had been turning towards the lifts, but now he swung back. 'Are you intending to go out?'

She was not so wimpish that she would just sit around waiting for him to look after her! 'Well, I'm not intending to stay inside the hotel for the whole of our visit!'

'No. Of course not. But . . . '

'Ben, I'm a modern woman,' she said firmly, 'and I often go out without a minder.' In Upper Shenstead. Which wasn't exactly a humming centre of activity. But the principle was the same. Wasn't it?

'I'll go and get some money changed for you, then.'

'I have my own money.'

'Don't be silly, Megan! You'll need more than that.'

Anger surged up again. Did the women he had known sit around and wait for handouts? Well, she wasn't going to. 'I won't need more, actually! There's a group excursion going out for a tour of the main sights tonight, and then on to a restaurant for dinner. It's not very expensive. Miss Barreth is going, so I won't be alone. I'll go and book on that.' Determined to show him how independent she was, she turned to wave at her former companion, mouthing the words, 'Wait for me!'

The older woman nodded.

'I'll go and book for you, then,' he said brusquely.

She was surprised as well as annoyed at his insistence. 'Ben, I'm quite capable of managing things like that for myself!'

'I know you are, but I have to go and get some money changed for myself and I can book your excursion at the same time.' He hesitated. 'I didn't mean to sound over-protective, truly. I'll see you up in our room shortly.'

She watched him walk across the lobby. When wearing his public persona, he looked sleek, well groomed and ready to kill. She could see women's eyes turning to follow his progress.

She much preferred him in relaxed mode, but she realised suddenly that she'd only seen him looking relaxed a few times. Since she joined him in London, he'd more often looked like this.

Her heart sank. Was this to be the pattern of their lives? Formality and separation, with an occasional relaxed patch in between? Ben said he'd sold his company, but his business interests still seemed to dominate his life, even on his honeymoon.

I'm being unfair, she told herself. He can't renegue on his previous arrangements. Squaring her shoulders, she walked briskly across for a word with Miss Barreth, who was delighted to have a companion on the sightseeing trip.

When Ben came up to their room, they were polite to one another but a little cool as they changed for their respective outings. The suit he donned this time was a light cream in colour, but no less formal than his dark ones, and with his hair sleeked down and his expression impersonal, he seemed like a different man entirely.

That man didn't even attempt to kiss her goodbye and this upset her most of all. Had she married a myth of her own creation? Had she been completely mistaken about Ben Saunders' true nature? The thought sent a pang through her. Surely not? No, that was just disappointment colouring her thoughts.

She finished getting ready, telling herself that she mustn't become paranoid. As he had said, these meetings had all been arranged before he even met her. Of course he couldn't cancel them.

But she couldn't help wishing he had done.

Megan didn't get back until quite late. It had turned out to be a fascinating evening for someone who had never visited Asia before. As she returned the greetings of the reception staff and took the lift, she was still bubbling with excitement about the temple they'd visited, the harbour at night and the food she'd eaten.

To her surprise, she found Ben waiting for her in their room. He'd changed into casual slacks and a short-sleeved top, but he didn't seem to be in a good mood. In fact, he scowled and made no attempt to walk across the room to greet her.

She paused in the doorway, her smile fading at the sight of the expression on his face. 'Oh! Have you been waiting long? I thought you'd be later than this.'

His voice was quite curt. 'I managed to get away early. I confided to my Chinese friend that I was on my honeymoon and he told the others. As a result we got through the business quite quickly by their standards.'

He'd been so disappointed to find the suite empty, with only her perfume lingering in the air to tantalise him that he'd grown angry with himself. He had no intention of getting dependent upon anyone, not even a wife. That way lay danger. Wiser to steer clear of intense emotions. Who should know that better than he?

But even so he had not been able to get the memory of their embraces out of his mind. How warm and willing Megan was, how responsive! And how unlike any woman he had ever known before!

As he'd waited in the hotel suite he'd been unable to settle to anything, and had simply sat there, listening for her. He'd felt ridiculously happy when he heard her stop outside the door and fumble with her key card, then had been afraid to reveal his feelings.

'What exactly is your business, Ben? You've never really talked about it.'

'It's partly import and export. I also manage some mixed deals, property, shares, things like that.'

'And what was tonight about?'

Frustration exploded out of him. 'Who the hell cares what tonight was about? You and I are supposed to be on our honeymoon!'

As he strode across to where she was standing, he looked so angry she couldn't help flinching. He grasped hold of her arm and pulled her towards him and she felt a tremor run through her. This kiss was nothing like the others. It was savage, dominating and as powerful as storm waves crashing on a beach. Within seconds she was kissing him back just as hungrily.

He paused to glare down fiercely at her. 'I don't care how tired you are, I intend to make love to you tonight.'

He was going too fast. She felt panic rising. 'Ben, I don't . . .'

His mouth smothered the rest of the sentence and as her dress fell to the ground, he dragged off the elaborate bedspread in one swift movement and tossed it aside, then turned to her, his eyes gleaming. 'Not ready yet? You're behaving like a virgin about to be ravished,' he teased.

'I . . . um, I am a virgin.'

He had been about to pull her down with him onto the

bed, but at that remark, he suddenly grabbed her shoulders and held her away from him. 'What did you say?'

She could feel herself going even redder and buried her face in the nearest thing, which happened to be his chest.

'Megan - we never talked about it - but are you really a virgin?'

She nodded, still avoiding his eyes.

His arms slackened for a moment. 'I never even gave the possibility a thought!'

'Does it matter?'

'Of course it matters!' Hell, he couldn't remember ever making love to a virgin. It put upon him the responsibility to make love to her even more carefully, to ensure that she was ripe and ready before he gained his own satisfaction.

And the idea of being the first filled him with an aching tenderness that seemed to intensify every feeling and response.

He stared at her unhappy, flushed face and pulled her back into his arms. 'Come here, you idiot, and kiss me again!' Holding her close, he murmured in her ear, 'There's nothing at all wrong with being a virgin, Megan. I was just surprised, that's all. In this day and age one doesn't expect such a precious gift from one's wife.'

Precious gift! Relief surged through her. He didn't mind, then. 'I hope I - I won't disappoint you,' she whispered, raising one hand hesitantly to stroke his face, then run it over his firm skin.

'I don't think you could disappoint me, Megan.'

Afterwards, she lay in his arms, drowsy but happy. 'I didn't know it could be like that. It was wonderful.'

He chuckled.

She was glad, now, that she had waited, though her virginity had been a secret cause of shame for years, forcing her to pretend an understanding of sex she didn't have when her cousin Sarah's conversations grew too confidential.

Megan had read books about making love, of course she had, but to know what happened between a man and a woman was one thing, to experience it quite another, she decided happily.

Ben's arms were loosening.

'I'm exhausted, wench. It's hard work ravishing virgins. You'll have to let me sleep now.'

Megan lay and listened to his breathing as it deepened and slowed down. It was a while before she could join him in sleep, because after they had made love, she had realised suddenly just why he could rouse her so easily.

She'd been fooling herself. All the time. Ever since that very first weekend. Hiding from the truth, in fact. But she wasn't going to hide from it any longer. She'd fallen in love with him, this self-contained, arrogant man who scorned the very idea of romance!

Only he was also a tender, thoughtful lover. He was kind and acted in a loving manner, to her, to his aunt as well.

She was stunned by the realisation of how she felt and hoped desperately that she hadn't betrayed her feelings while they were making love, because she was not sure how he would react to the idea of her loving him.

He had made it more than plain from the beginning that he didn't want or believe in romance, only friendship and loyalty.

But couldn't help loving him. Wanted to tell him, to say it aloud, to revel in it.

And didn't dare.

She would have to be careful to say none of the words of love that rose to her lips so easily.

She frowned. And what about him? Not once in all the time they'd been together had he used even the slightest endearment, not even when they were making love. He had spoken her name, called her wench, said she was beautiful, but nothing else.

And suddenly she wanted endearments. She wanted the whole damn thing. She felt bewildered by the strength of her own emotions and yet terrified of driving him away from her by revealing them.

At least they were married now and she could be with him, whether he loved her now or not. She must be very patient. Surely he would grow fond of her in time? She knew he liked her. She did have that, at least.

It was a strange thought for a bride, but then, theirs was a strange union.

Rubbish! a last sleepy thought drifted through her mind. That sharp little voice in her head again. You're still fooling yourself, Megan Saunders. What you really want now is for him to love you. As much as you love him.

Was she a fool to hope for that? She didn't know. She prayed not.

She didn't think she'd be satisfied with mere liking and friendship, not for the rest of her life anyway, not from the man whose children she wanted to bear one day.

The next two days passed in a whirl of shopping and sightseeing, with Ben only attending two very brief business meetings. Apart from that they spent every minute together and for most of the time, it was in every sense a honeymoon.

The only thing missing was that the bridegroom still did not use any endearments and the bride was careful to follow suit. And why it mattered so much to her, Megan couldn't have said. But it did matter. Details like that seemed very important indeed in a long-term relationship.

But passion was there, at least, sometimes seeming to float through the air that separated the two of them, igniting at the most unlikely moments and always bringing intense pleasure to them both.

'We are,' he said one day, 'incredibly well suited sexually.'

'Yes.' She held her breath, hoping he'd say something tender, but he just murmured sleepily in her ear that she had a gorgeous body and snuggled up to her.

Don't expect instant miracles, Megan, she told herself as she lay waiting for sleep to wipe away that moisture brimming in her eyes. No one promised you miracles. Just take it one day at a time. Don't be greedy. Be thankful for what you've got, which is more than you've ever had before.

But with every day that passed she did want more, wanted it quite desperately.

Chapter 8

The relatively short, five-hour flight from Singapore to Western Australia seemed to pass quickly, but Megan could tell that Ben was thinking of business again as they collected their luggage at Perth airport.

That tight expression on his face was beginning to seem like a gate that kept slamming into place between them, and when he was in that mode, he seemed to think of nothing else but the task in hand.

A large chauffeur-driven vehicle was waiting for them again at the airport and they were whisked away towards the city. Traffic was heavy, with huge trucks thundering past them, and the road was lined with garish business signs and commercial buildings.

He glanced at her and smiled. 'Disappointed?'

'Well . . . ' she hesitated, looking up at the lowering skies, ' . . . I thought Australia would be - you know - sunny.'

'It's winter, when we get most of our rain. It'll probably be sunny tomorrow, part of the time, anyway. It rarely stays dull for long.' He leaned forward and spoke to the driver. 'Before you deliver us to the hotel, would you please take us along Riverside Drive and up to King's Park.'

'That's the new casino.' He pointed to a lumpy geometrical building. 'And on the other side of the river you can see the city block.'

'Skyscrapers!' She was so disappointed. To her, having grown up in a cosy village surrounded by neat fields and farms, skyscrapers were an urban obscenity. 'What river is that?'

'The Swan. In summer, there are boats and yachts everywhere and at night the water reflects the city lights. It can be very pretty. I asked for a hotel suite looking out towards it.'

She nodded. Now he was neither lover, nor businessman, but had changed into a courteous stranger.

And she didn't like the change, not at all.

When the car stopped in King's Park, he helped her out then raised her hand to his lips and kissed it formally. 'Welcome to Perth, Mrs Saunders.'

She'd rather he'd kissed her lips. She'd rather he'd not had that abstracted look in his eyes. Oh, you're such a fool, she told herself. Will you just stop wishing for the moon. 'Can we have a short walk?'

They strolled along towards a lookout perched on the edge of a small cliff overlooking the city and widest part of the river. Below them was a freeway buzzing with traffic and beyond that a wide stretch of water. What looked like a ferry was moving slowly from one side to the other.

Megan linked her arm in Ben's and spoke with determined cheerfulness. 'This must be one of the most beautiful locations for a city in the world.'

'I think so,' he said quietly, nodding at it as if greeting an old friend. 'I've grown to love it.'

But she wished he hadn't spoiled the moment by glancing at his watch.

'I'll bring you up here again one evening, Megan, so that you can see the city lights, but at the moment, I need to get to the hotel. Apart from the fact that it's about to pour down, I'm expecting a few messages from New York.'

'When are we going to your house in the country?'

'Our house, now.'

'Sorry, our house.' But it wouldn't feel like her house until had seen it. And she didn't really want to go to another hotel. It seemed very important that they have a real home together. 'When can we go there?'

He hesitated. 'Well, in a day or two, perhaps. I have some people to see first. In the meantime, I expect you'll enjoy going round the shops.'

She let out an exasperated puff of air at his tone, which seemed more suitable to a child about to be consoled for something by new toys. 'Actually, I'm not mad keen on shopping.'

'Wonders will never cease! A woman who's not obsessed

by clothes.'

That did it! She let go of his arm and faced him, hands on hips. 'I don't appreciate patronising remarks, thank you very much.'

'It wasn't - '

'Oh, yes, it was! And it's worse if you don't even know when you're being patronising. Not all woman are obsessed by shopping, you know.' She led the way to the car at a smart pace, not even looking behind to see if he were following.

They got back inside in dead silence. His face was expressionless and he sat down at the opposite end of the seat with plenty of space between them. As they drove along he made no attempt to bridge the gap.

Well, she wasn't going to make the first move, she decided, anger still simmering through her.

At the hotel there was the usual obsequious service which Ben seemed to generate out of nowhere. 'Another bridal suite?' she asked in the lift.

'Is there something wrong with bridal suites?'

'They're a bit overpowering, that's all. Fussy.'

The rest of the journey up was accomplished in a silence so heavy you could almost have weighed it.

Their suite was another impersonal essay in opulence and Megan's nose wrinkled scornfully as she looked around.

'I don't understand you,' Ben said abruptly. 'I thought you'd enjoy this sort of thing. After all, you've had a - well, a rather restricted life so far.'

'I did enjoy the luxury hotels at first. But now I'd rather have a home of our own.' And a husband who didn't have half his mind on business when they'd only just arrived in Australia and she was dying to get out and see something.

'Have I upset you?'

'Of course you have! You were treating me like a child, some idiot who could be made happy by presents.'

He ran his hand through his hair. 'I'm sorry. I really

didn't mean it to sound like that.'

Suddenly he was Ben again, not the cool businessman. And Megan realised how ridiculous she'd been, expecting him to understand instinctively what she wanted. 'I suppose I was just - well, disappointed that we weren't going to our home.'

He came across and pulled her towards him, bending his head to kiss her. But this time she pulled back. 'Don't!'

'Why not? You usually like it.'

'Because it seems to be your answer to everything. Make love to her and then she'll forget whatever it is that's upset her.' Unfortunately, she did forget. In fact, she went into meltdown the minute his lips touched hers. So she wasn't going to let him do that to her, not when she had a point to make.

He swung away abruptly, his expression grim. 'I've no intention of forcing myself upon you. Perhaps you'll put up a sign when I am allowed near you!'

She bit back a sharp remark and turned towards their suitcases.

While she unpacked their things and changed, he went through the letters and faxes that were piled near the phone. 'Nothing here that can't wait.' He hesitated. 'Shall we - would you like to go down and have a cocktail in the lobby? I wouldn't mind an early dinner. You usually seem to like watching people.'

It sounded like an olive branch and she seized it gladly. 'I'd enjoy that.' She went over and linked her arm in his. 'Come on, then, take your grumpy old wife out and feed her.'

He stared at her solemnly. 'I didn't mean to be patronising, Megan. Truly I didn't.'

'And I think I over-reacted. Let's forget it.'

They were laughing together as they came out of the lift, then Ben stopped dead in his tracks and she felt his whole body become tense.

What now?

She followed his glance, to see a woman staring across at them. After a moment's hesitation, the stranger waved and began to cross the lobby. She was tall and extremely elegant, but her expression could only be described as sexually aware. The admiring glances she received from one or two men showed clearly that she had made an impact on them and the half smile on her face betrayed her enjoyment of this.

As soon as the stranger spoke Megan recognised Cynthia from their one short telephone conversation. Impossible to mistake that affected drawl.

'Ben, dahhh-ling!'

He took the hand that was reaching greedily towards him and shook it briefly, keeping her at arm's length.

Cynthia tossed back her shoulder-length blonde hair and made a moue at him, completely ignoring Megan. 'So formal, Ben?'

'Cynthia, I'd like you to meet my wife. Megan, this is an old acquaintance of mine, Cynthia Berevic.'

'Friend, not acquaintance, surely, Ben. We've known each other for absolutely years.' Cynthia waved a hand vaguely in Megan's direction, but continued to address her remarks to him. 'I heard you'd got married. Everyone was so-o-o surprised.'

She paused to stare at Megan for a few seconds, as if she were something that had crawled out from under a stone and should have stayed there, then turned back to Ben. 'No one knew you had a thing going.'

'Why should they? It was no one else's business.'

Sneaking a quick glance at her husband, Megan decided he was not happy to see Cynthia. Good. At least - she hoped that was what was making him frown. Louisa had said the Berevics lived in Sydney. Why couldn't they have stayed there?

An older man with a drawn face came across to join them and his arrival caused Ben to smile with genuine warmth. 'Nick!'

While the two men thumped each other on the back a few times, Cynthia totally ignored Megan, who studied a nearby mural, hoping she looked interested in it.

Nick's voice had a slight accent to it. 'Didn't know you were back in Australia, Ben.'

'Just flew in today. How are you keeping? Really, Nick? Recovering all right?'

'Oh, yes. Can't keep me down for long. It was only a minor heart attack. But I still have to take things easy for a while.' He looked at Megan questioningly.

'Nick, this is my wife. We were married last week in London. Megan, this is Nick Berevic, a business colleague of mine and a good friend. Nick helped me a lot when I first came to Australia.'

'You didn't need much help, my friend, just a few introductions.' Unlike his wife Nick shook Megan's hand warmly, keeping it clasped in his for a minute as he studied her. 'I hope you'll both be very happy. You'll forgive an old man for saying how fresh and beautiful your face is, Megan.'

'Thank you.' She liked him on the spot. He had all the warmth and charm his wife lacked. She noticed that Cynthia's expression had turned sour at her husband's compliment, then the other woman recovered and started to smile at Ben again.

'Well, you certainly made up your mind quickly this time, dahh-ling. I didn't know you'd met anyone so - er,' she cast a disbelieving look sideways, 'special.'

He spoke quietly, turning to put his arm round Megan. 'One day was all it took before we decided to get married.'

Was she mistaken, Megan wondered, or was there an appeal for help in his eyes? 'No, it was one and a half days, actually,' she joked, backing him up without hesitation. 'And our first meeting was definitely - unusual.'

'It was indeed. She rushed across the hotel foyer and tackled a pickpocket who'd just stolen my wallet. Quite a reversal of roles - heroine saves hero.'

Ben's chuckle was quite genuine and made Cynthia press her lips together and eye Megan from head to toes, as if she couldn't believe there was anything special about her. Megan returned Cynthia stare for stare and cuddled up to her husband as she did so.

Nick, who didn't seem to have noticed the subtle undertones, clapped Ben on the shoulder, a familiar fatherly gesture. 'Well, it's great to see you two love birds, but if you've just arrived from England, you must be exhausted. We haven't all got Cynthia's splendid constitution. She arrived a couple of days ago, but she never seems to suffer from jet lag.'

He looked at his wife so proudly and Cynthia looked so disinterested that Megan thought suddenly, I pity him! I can't see her being a comfort to someone who's not well.

Cynthia took her husband's arm, but it was Ben whom she addressed. 'I'm very cross with you, you know. You didn't even invite me to the wedding.'

'I didn't know you were in London.'

Megan was amazed at how straight he kept his face as he said this.

'Oh?' Cynthia's tone showed her disbelief. 'But I left a message for you on your office number and at your aunt's.'

'Things were chaotic as we were closing down. And my aunt must have forgotten to pass the message on. Anyway, the wedding wasn't a lavish production. Just family and a few old school friends.'

As he made a move to leave, Cynthia reached out to grab his arm. 'I must say, you don't look to be overcome with exhaustion.' Her voice took on a coaxing purr. 'Why don't you two have dinner with us tonight? We're only in Perth for a few days while Nick closes a deal, and it'd be lovely to catch up with you again.'

Nick patted his wife's hand as it lay on his arm. 'I must say, I think that's an excellent idea. Not if you're too tired, of course.'

Megan could feel her husband's tension in the arm that still lay around her shoulders. Why? Because he was still attracted to that woman? Or because he didn't want to spend time with her? It suddenly seemed rather important to know which, yet she knew she couldn't ask him.

Oh, she was getting so tired of treading carefully all the time!

'We won't take no for an answer,' said Cynthia firmly. 'You were obviously going out somewhere to eat and it might as well be with us. How about a cocktail before dinner? Nick's hardly seen anyone for ages. Convalescence is so tedious. It'll do him good to chat with an old friend.' She smiled rather too sweetly at Megan. 'Not to mention making a new one.'

What's the woman up to? Megan wondered, as Ben squeezed her shoulder and accepted for them both.

She'd have said no and eaten in their room.

After a cocktail, they dined in the hotel restaurant. The meal seemed interminable to Megan. She chatted, tried to smile, listened to talk about people who meant nothing to her. And gradually she began to wonder whether Cynthia wasn't doing this on purpose.

At one stage, when she was feeling as though she could not bear this meaningless chat for another second longer, she excused herself to go to the ladies' room. You're not in that woman's league, she told her face in the mirror. Dear Cynthia absolutely oozes elegance and wealth. I bet she does nothing but buy clothes when her husband's busy.

As Megan patted her unruly hair into place, she shook her head. A real country bumpkin, that's what you are, Megan Ross. Then she mentally corrected herself. No, she was Megan Saunders now and must not forget that. Nor must she allow Cynthia to forget it.

She sighed and searched the mirror again, feeling she ought to look different now she was married. But she didn't. Same old rosy, unsophisticated face.

A favourite saying of her uncle's came back to her, No

use pretending to be what you're not, my girl. You may fool everyone else, but you won't fool yourself. Yes, she thought, but I can't remain a simple country girl now, not married to a man like Ben Saunders. I'll have to do some adapting if we're to have a good life together.

And so will he!

As she was walking back towards the restaurant, all her good resolutions to appear more sophisticated vanished, for when she looked across the lobby, Nick was also missing from the table and Ben was sitting holding Cynthia's hand. A raging fury filled Megan and she stopped dead. How dared he hold hands with another woman after all he had said about loyalty? She sucked in a couple of painful breaths, then swung round and strode back across the foyer.

She would not confront him now. She didn't intend to make a public spectacle of herself! But she wasn't going to rejoin them. No way!

Once in their suite she phoned the reception desk. 'Could you please give a message to my husband? Ben Saunders. He's sitting at a corner table in the foyer bar with a blond woman. Tell him I've retired to our suite with a sudden migraine. Thank you.'

She slammed down the phone and threw off the expensive new dress, kicking it into a corner, heedless of whether it got damaged. 'I can always shop for more, after all!' she snarled at it.

She went for a shower, but although the warmth of the water was soothing on her body, it didn't ease her anger. She scrubbed away the tears fiercely, but more kept falling.

When she came out of the bathroom, Ben was sitting in an armchair, arms folded, looking just as furious as she felt.

She didn't wait for him to speak. 'I didn't expect you back so soon!'

'Nick isn't allowed any late nights.'

'You could have stayed on with your dear friend

Cynthia!'

He jerked to his feet. 'I didn't want to stay with her. But I did expect you to have more manners than just to vanish without so much as a word of apology.'

'You shouldn't sit there holding some other woman's hand, then! I didn't like to interrupt your cosy little tête-à-tête.'

'She was holding my hand, actually.'

'Well, you weren't exactly pulling yours away!' Megan sat down at the dressing table and began to brush her hair, sending it crackling into a halo around her face.

The brush was removed from her hand and she was pulled to her feet. She didn't resist, but she did not attempt to soften the furious expression on her face, either.

'Do I detect some jealousy there, Mrs Saunders?'

She looked at the hand holding her wrist. 'Do you mind?'

He didn't let go, just took hold of her other wrist and pulled her closer to him. A thrill ran through her, but she didn't answer, couldn't find the breath, somehow.

His voice became lower, softer. 'I asked you a question. Would you answer it, please?'

She was still filled with anger. She had been altogether too meek since they got married. Well, that was over now. So Ben was rich! Well, money wasn't everything. She had got to stop letting it worry her and - and just get on with living. And he was the one who'd made such a parade of needing loyalty from a wife.

'I must admit,' she said, articulating her words with care, 'that I don't enjoy dining with my husband's former mistress. Who would? And I feel sorry for that nice man who's married to her. She probably drove him to the heart attack.'

'You are jealous!' He sounded surprised.

'I'm not!' A tearful snort escaped her control and as she felt his eyes on her, she shrugged and tried to blink the tears away. But they wouldn't go, so she smeared them away with her fingers, muttering, 'Well, any wife would be.'

'Cynthia's not my mistress now. And it was a very brief affair. Strangely enough, I'm the one who introduced her to Nick.'

'I bet she got the grappling hooks out as soon as she saw his bank balance!'

Ben opened his mouth then shut it again. That was an uncomfortably accurate summary of how Cynthia had reacted to Nick's open admiration. 'You're right. He's a lot richer than I am.'

Megan couldn't help asking, 'Why didn't you marry her yourself? She's certainly a luscious piece!'

He scowled at her. 'Cynthia always knew I wasn't interested in marriage. I made that plain from the start of our relationship. I didn't consider her – still don't – wife material.'

'Then why did you marry me? I don't fit into your world. I'm an even less suitable wife for a man like you.'

His voice softened. 'Because I wanted to marry you - very much - as I never wanted to marry Cynthia. Apart from the physical attraction, you and I both want the same things from a marriage.'

Megan sighed. She wasn't sure she found this explanation satisfying but didn't dare push him any further, not with that closed look still on his face. They'd trodden through enough emotional quicksands today. One step at a time, she said to herself. That was becoming her watchword. 'Well, I know you like Nick, but just don't expect me even to pretend to be friendly with Cynthia! She's definitely not my type.'

'A little common civility is all I ask. Surely that shouldn't be too difficult?'

Megan flushed and couldn't think what to say in response to that, aware that she had let her temper rule her head tonight.

He drew her slowly towards him, his eyes searching hers. 'Let's forget Cynthia, hmm? She really isn't important.' His voice was husky as he added, 'I've been looking forward all evening to getting you alone.'

She stared up at him, not sure she liked the way he could turn her bones to rubber, still struggling against it. 'Why?'

His hands became still. 'What do you mean, why?'

'Why were you looking forward to it? Am I a good bed partner?'

'The best.'

'Well, that's something, I suppose.'

But he still hadn't used any endearments with her. And that was beginning to matter, to fret away at her hopes for the future. If his lips had not been so close she might have told him to leave her alone tonight, but one kiss and she forgot her anger.

Soon they were both lost to the world.

Only afterwards did she wonder if she was always going to be so susceptible to his touch. But a smile crept across her face at that thought. Surely she had just proved that he was equally susceptible to her touch, proved it to her complete and utter satisfaction?

It was another step along the way she wanted to tread. It had to be!

She just had to be patient.

Chapter 9

The following day Ben had to attend more meetings. 'Just a few more, then that part of my life will be over,' he explained.

Determined to remain cheerful, Megan nodded. After he had left, she went out on her own to explore Perth, delighted to find it sunny if cool today. She lifted her face to the sun, enjoying the warmth. And although it was winter, she had no need of a coat, which seemed absolutely miraculous after English winters.

The city centre was criss-crossed by walkways and shopping malls, which created a world apart from the traffic. She particularly liked Forrest Place, where preparations were being made for a midday concert in the open air and where, even in winter, it was warm enough for people to sit outside at tables and chat over cups of coffee. She joined them, sipping her coffee and watching the passers-by.

Still feeling faintly defiant after Ben's gibes about shopping, she decided to buy books not clothes. Once she was inside a book shop, the last traces of her anger evaporated and as always she lost herself in the sheer pleasure of browsing through the rows of colourful volumes that tempted her fingers to reach out for them, touch them, open them, buy just one more. For the first time she used the credit card Ben had provided, signing her new married name with a smile.

When she came out of the bookshop, she continued to stroll along. In one mall there was a stand where people were collecting money to save endangered species. She made a contribution, feeling it a good way to start life in Australia, then got talking to the guy handing out leaflets. They compared notes about what was being done in her part of England and what needed to be done here, and half an hour had passed before she realised it.

By the time she moved on, she had volunteered to join

their efforts and he'd given her an application form.

Since it was now lunch time she hurried back to the hotel, her heart lifting at the thought of meeting Ben as they'd arranged. She felt guilty for being late, but found the room empty, with only a brief message pushed under the door saying Mr Saunders had been unavoidably detained on business and would get back as soon as he could after lunch.

'Oh, and I'm just to wait around again, am I?' Megan exclaimed, feeling bitterly disappointed. She had been looking forward to Ben's company in the afternoon, had wanted to share what she had found out and do some further exploring together.

And she didn't like the brusque tone of the note or the way he kept issuing what sounded like orders. She screwed up the paper and let it drop to the floor. 'Well, sorry, Mr Saunders, but you won't find me sitting here meekly waiting until you deign to return!'

She flicked through the brochures she'd picked up in the hotel lobby and found she could cruise down the river to somewhere called Fremantle. Good! She'd vanish for the afternoon and if Ben came back when he said he would, she'd let him sit around wondering where she had gone, for a change!

The desk clerk gave her instructions for finding the cruise-boat terminal, but she refused his offer to call a taxi because she needed a brisk walk to use up some of her energy.

As she passed a sign indicating a shopping precinct, she decided to go inside and buy herself a sandwich. By this time she had walked off some of her anger and was wondering whether to return to the hotel. Perhaps she had over-reacted. Well, she knew she had over-reacted. Her feelings for Ben seemed to be see-sawing up and down all the time.

She rode down the escalator into a basement shopping mall, looking around her with great interest. Half the city's shops seemed to be underground or indoors. Was that because of the hot summers?

Part of the way down, however, she gasped aloud and shock held her so rigid that she would have fallen off at the bottom had it not been for the quick support of a woman behind her.

Murmuring a hurried thank you, she ducked behind a pillar, flushing as the woman turned round to stare at her in open-mouthed amazement.

After a moment Megan peered carefully out. Yes, there they were, sitting in an intimate huddle at a table outside a café - her husband and Cynthia! They hadn't noticed her, so engrossed were they in earnest conversation. She stood there watching them, fuming. It was disgusting the way that woman kept pawing Ben! And even more disgusting that he kept allowing it!

Swallowing hard, Megan tried to keep her emotions under control, but tears filled her eyes. From the look of things, Ben wasn't finished with Cynthia. Perhaps he wanted to have his cake and eat it?

Well, Megan wasn't going to put up with that. Definitely not!

After a minute or two she managed to pull herself together and stepped back on the escalator, resentment sizzling through her. She wondered if he'd notice her. But of course there was no shout from behind her because he hadn't eyes for anything but Cynthia.

So he had been detained on business, had he? What business could he possibly have with her? All that talk in England about faithfulness and loyalty within marriage! What he meant was that his wife must be loyal, while he did as he pleased. The usual male double standard and she had fallen for it, hook, line and sinker!

More by luck than good management, she found her way down to the ferries. Once on board she gazed out at the Swan River with lacklustre eyes, unable to get the picture of her husband and Cynthia cosying up at the table out of her mind.

At one stage in the slow journey down the river, she noticed a man looking at her admiringly. He gave her a friendly nod and she glared at him, feeling a surge of satisfaction as he hurriedly looked elsewhere. She didn't flirt with other men. Didn't want to.

Pain filled her and tears welled in her eyes. All she wanted was for her husband to love her. Would that be too much to ask?

She was sure she and Ben were well suited - or at least, they could be if he would give it a real chance. If he would only let affection grow between them, they could build a home and a wonderful life together. She lost herself for a while in dreams of what that home might be like, what a child of Ben's might look like, then jerked back into cold reality as she realised they had just reached Fremantle.

So upset was she that she even considered getting off the boat and staying out all evening, just to emphasise her independence, but that urge was short-lived. It would gain her nothing to behave irrationally. Besides, there might just be some reasonable explanation, at least on Ben's part. She hoped there was, though she couldn't think of one at the moment.

What was plain was that Cynthia was making every effort to re-engage his attention.

What wasn't plain to Megan was what he really wanted.

As she thought about it, she frowned and tried to picture the pair of them, realising suddenly that there had been nothing lover-like in his expression or body language as he sat in the mall. It was Cynthia who'd been leaning forward and pawing him.

Was that just her own wishful thinking? No, now that she was feeling calmer, she didn't think so. Oh, dear, had her anger blinded her?

In any case, it was time to get back to the hotel. She had made her point by now. If there was a point. She felt so confused she didn't know any more.

The return journey up the river seemed to take for ever and the sky had clouded over again. The scenery was beautiful, with large homes set among grey-green gum trees on the low slopes overlooking the river. The occasional boat went chugging past, bobbing round the wide curves of water in a leisurely way. In other circumstances she would have been delighted with it all, but it was a relief when the trip was over. She wasn't in the mood to appreciate scenery today.

She walked slowly back along the foreshore towards the hotel and when she got close, she sat down on one of the benches by the river and admitted to herself that she was reluctant to face Ben. Ignoring the cold wind that promised more rain, ignoring the fact that dusk was falling fast, she stared across the water and admitted it.

She'd over-reacted.

I am jealous, she decided. Ben was right about that. Only she loved him so much.

But what sort of love was this where she couldn't even tell him how she felt, couldn't even complain about him having lunch with another woman? Sniffing away a tear, she blew her nose determinedly. She must be totally stupid to have got herself into this.

She stared blindly at the expanse of water and sighed. No, she wasn't stupid. How could she not have fallen in love with him? It was more than a physical thing, for her at least. She remembered how happy they'd been together in Singapore, how much fun they'd had, how she'd enjoyed simple things like chatting to him or just walking along hand in hand.

Misery swept through her. Their delicate situation had gone from bad to worse since their arrival in Perth.

She balled up the soggy tissue and fumbled for another. Well, she decided, she'd accepted his conditions about marriage, so she couldn't complain that she hadn't known what she was getting into. And maybe he might grow fond of her over the years.

A tear slid down her cheek. She didn't want fondness. She wanted romance, passion. Fierce hot lovemaking, yes, but on a foundation of love. And she didn't want to wait years for it, either.

Rain, hunger and darkness drove her back to the hotel. All she had managed to decide by then was that she must continue to be cool and pleasant with him as he was with her. As for Cynthia, Megan intended to wait and see what happened before she said or did anything more about that woman.

If she could force herself to wait.

If she didn't lose her temper first.

He had never seen her lose her temper. She didn't give in to it nowadays, though she had as a child. But then, during the past few years what reason had she had to go into a red rage? None. She had made sure of that. Lived a quiet life. Avoided things that might be painful.

When she entered their suite, he bounced to his feet and glared at her, hands on hips. 'Where the hell have you been?'

'Out.' Delighted with this reaction, she took off her jacket and shook the raindrops from it, avoiding his eyes. She was glad he was angry. Serve him bloody right! He never told her where he was going, so why should she always have to tell him?

He moved across to her, opened his mouth to say something, then closed it and stretched out one hand to feel the jacket. 'You're soaked!'

She spread the jacket carefully over the back of a nearby chair, still avoiding looking directly at him. 'Yes. And I'm feeling quite chilled, so I think I'll take a nice hot shower. That'll warm me up.'

He followed her into the bathroom, barring her way to the shower. 'You still haven't said where you've been.'

Briefly she considered refusing to tell him, then shrugged. 'I've been on a boat trip to Fremantle. It's a beautiful river, isn't it?'

'What on earth made you do that?'

'You weren't here, I didn't know when you'd be returning and I was fed up of shopping. Fed up of hotel rooms, too.'

'But we agreed you'd wait here for me! I sent a message to say I'd be back after lunch and I was.'

She could see that he was controlling his temper only with an effort, but she was beyond caring whether she upset him. He'd upset her twice in the past twenty-four hours. 'I'm getting a little tired of waiting for you in hotel rooms, Ben. And we didn't agree to anything. You gave orders, told me what to do. Since I didn't agree and you don't always return when you say you will, I decided to go out on my own.'

He scowled at her. 'I've been worried sick about you. Perth, like every other large city, has its share of muggings and crime, you know.'

She shrugged again. 'I thought you didn't want a clinging wife. I distinctly recall you telling me that.' She started taking her clothes off.

'I'd prefer to know where my wife is, especially when she's out after dark in a strange city. You left no message, you know, not a single word.'

'Sorry. I forgot.' She turned on the water and stepped into the shower, effectively cutting off further questions. A few tears slid down her face, but by dint of concentrating on her grievances, she managed to stop her stupid tendency to weep.

The shower screen opened and a naked body joined her under the water. 'Oh, hell, Megan, I missed you this afternoon!'

'Did you really?' She stared at him through a blur of spray. He seemed to fill the whole shower space. A shiver of excitement ran down her spine and the antagonism started to fade.

'Of course I missed you!' He pulled her into his arms and kissed her wet face. 'Here, let me wash your back.' He took the soap out of her hand, turned her gently round and began to wash her body with slow, sensuous movements.

She felt bewildered. He was behaving as if he really did care about her. Why didn't he say something affectionate, then?

When he pulled her against him, she lost the battle to think.

Dropping the soap, he trapped her in the corner, took her face in his hands and pinned her to the tiles with a thrust of his lean hips, rocking against her belly, his arousal an urgent throb against her softness.

'Stop,' she muttered half-heartedly.

'Why should we?' he demanded. 'Your body shows you're enjoying it as much as I am.'

She tried to wriggle out of his grasp, but the way he was standing made it impossible. 'Ben, I . . . ' she began, but his mouth covered hers and stopped any further protests.

Suddenly there seemed to be only the two of them and the warm hissing water in the whole world. She sighed and put her arms round him, leaning her wet face against the damp skin of his shoulder and blinking the water from her eyes. 'Oh, Ben, I only went out because I was so fed up,' she confessed. 'I was missing you, too.'

He turned off the taps and drew her towards the bed, cradling her in his arms and making love to her with exquisite tenderness. At least it felt like tenderness.

Or was it just skill?

Afterwards, she lay with her head against his chest and sighed.

'What's upsetting you, Megan?'

You are, she wanted to say. You've done it again, made love without using any words of affection. 'I'm getting a bit tired of hotels.'

It was part of the truth, at least. She knew she was a poor liar. 'I guess I'm the sort of person who needs a home and - and something to do with her days.' She didn't say anything about his meeting with Cynthia, because she couldn't bear to spoil the rapport between them.

'I'm tired of hotels, too, have been for a while.'

He said nothing for a few minutes and she couldn't think of anything to fill the silence with, so didn't try. He seemed quite relaxed and she could only hope that her own tension didn't show as she lay against the slow rise and fall of his chest.

'I have a confession to make,' he said at last.

It felt as if her heart had stopped beating for a moment or two and only a whisper of sound scraped out. 'What?'

'It's about my - our house.'

Relief flooded through her. She could not have borne the confession to be about Cynthia. 'They say it's good for the soul,' she managed at last.

'What is?'

'Confession.'

'Hmm. Well, here goes. I haven't built a proper house yet, so there's nowhere you'll really be able to call home. I've bought about two hundred acres of land fronting onto the Harvey Estuary. It's undeveloped bush, most of it. There's a house of sorts there, but it's only a tumble-down beach shack. I was going to live in it until I'd designed and built a much bigger house, then knock the shack down.'

'Sounds fun.'

He fell silent for a while. 'Perhaps we'd better rent a house somewhere. Here in Perth, or in Mandurah, if you like the town. I'd prefer Mandurah, I think. It's a seaside resort, not at all like the English ones, very Australian.'

'Couldn't we go and look at this shack, then decide afterwards? Surely you don't have business meetings every single day? Besides, I'd love to see what Western Australia is like, the real Western Australia, not this city.'

'Don't you like Perth?'

'I've only seen the city block and the river. And yes, I do like it. What's more, I met some people today who are trying to do something about endangered species.' She told him about the guy she had been talking to, about her intention of joining the group.

'I'll check them out for you, see if they're bona fide,' he said immediately after she'd finished.

'No, I'll check them out. As soon as I get on line, I can email some contacts in England. In the meantime I can tell whether people are amateurs or near professionals, you know.' She smiled. 'I really don't need you to act as watchdog over everything I do.'

He was silent, then admitted, 'I'd like to help with something like that as well. I am aware of the conservation issues, but I'd never really had time to do much about it, apart from making donations. But you can't avoid thinking about it these days and it does make sense to take better care of our environment.'

'Everyone should make some effort. And donations are needed as well as workers. But maybe, once you've sorted out the rest of your business dealings, you'll have time to do something in person?' She'd like that, working together.

He smiled. 'And I'm sure you're going to show me what to do.'

She couldn't help smiling back. 'Yes. I probably am, once I've got to know this country better. I bought a couple of books today. But,' she looked quickly sideways at him, feeling the need, as always, to gauge his mood before she revealed her own feelings, 'it would definitely have been more fun to go out together today.'

'I did send a message to say I was delayed.'

'Great! Mr Saunders is delayed. Suspend all activity until he beckons. I'm not like that, Ben. I like to keep busy.' She bit off more angry words. She must keep her temper in check. Their relationship was still too fragile to stand any real stress. His next remark both surprised and pleased her, however.

'I should have rung you personally. I'm sorry, Megan. I will next time.'

'I'd much prefer that.' Honesty compelled her to add,

'I'm just not - not used to this sort of dawdling life. I not only need something to do, I'd prefer it to be something worthwhile.'

She leaned across to kiss his cheek. His expression was unfathomable. He could hide his emotions better than anyone she had ever met, just switching them off in mid-sentence at times. When he spoke, however, he surprised her again.

'I hope you'll never get used to such a life. I admire your enthusiasm. I'm tying up the loose ends as quickly as I can, Megan, I promise you.'

She was surprised by the expression of distaste on his face. 'You sound as if you hate it.'

'Not hate it, no. But it would never have been my choice to go into this sort of business.'

'Why did you do it, then?'

'It was the family business. At the time, there were a couple of elderly cousins of my father's who had shares in it. They'd have been left penniless if I'd let the business fail. And I knew Aunt Louisa had invested rather heavily in it, too. Well, not invested, but lent my father some money, which amounted to the same thing, I suppose. He was her only brother, after all.'

There was a long pause, and he added in a bitter tone, 'There was also my mother to consider, you see. She'd have taken everything if I'd tried to close the business down. She has excellent lawyers and usually comes out of her marriages with a fistful of extra assets.'

'Marriages?'

'Yes. She's on her fourth husband now, but if I read the signs right, she's tiring of him.'

He scowled and it was a few moments before he added, 'Anyway, she put some money into my father's business when they were first married and her lawyers tied up her rights to repayment rather cleverly. My father hadn't really studied the contracts - he trusted her, I suppose. As it turned out, he was never able to pay her off. I have, though.'

She was surprised. And touched by his confidences. This was a rare glimpse behind his mask. 'Well, you certainly seem to have made a huge success of it all.'

'Yes. If a thing's worth doing, and all that . . . I'm financially independent now, thank goodness.'

He sighed as if that gave him little pleasure, then caught sight of the wall clock. 'Oh, damn! Look, I've agreed that we'll have dinner with Nick and Cynthia this evening. I suppose we'd better start getting dressed.'

The joy left her abruptly. 'Do we have to?'

'I'm afraid so.'

'I must admit I find Cynthia hard going.' Silence stretched between them. She was determined not to be the one who broke it.

'Yes. I realise that. But I'd be grateful if you'd make the effort to be polite to her, just this once. I owe Nick a lot and he's a very nice man, but he's not as well as he pretends. If I can help him in this matter, I'd like to.'

She shrugged. 'All right. We have to eat, I suppose. And we needn't stay up late, surely?'

'Definitely not. You're wearing me out. I need some sleep.'

She rolled over, intending to go and get dressed, but he pulled her back into his arms. She had expected one of his devouring kisses that set her whole body tingling, but he simply pressed his lips against her cheek and said softly, 'You have beautiful skin, Megan and I'd like to kiss every inch of it. Believe me, if I had my way, we'd stay here and order room service.' Then he put his hands on either side of her face and pressed another very gentle kiss on the tip of her nose. 'Come on, then, Mrs Saunders. Let's go and do our duty!'

Gentle as the last kiss had been, she could feel its imprint for several minutes and it had just as much effect on her as one of his passionate mouth-bruising kisses. More perhaps, because it offered the tenderness she craved.

But it occurred to her as she finished dressing that she'd wound up agreeing to do what he wanted. She always did. And, unless she mistook what was going on, he was getting better at managing her.

She didn't like being managed.

Cynthia and Nick were waiting for them in the foyer and Nick was looking very tired. Megan found herself paired off with him as they walked across to the restaurant while Cynthia draped herself possessively over Ben's arm and shoulder.

Gritting her teeth, Megan chatted to Nick with determined cheerfulness, keeping her eyes away from the others. Well, most of the time.

Throughout the meal, Cynthia continued to sparkle and address all her remarks to the two men. Megan decided there was an amusing side to all this - if you could keep yourself detached - if you didn't feel like scratching the other woman's eyes out. After all, Cynthia was working very hard indeed to keep herself the centre of the two men's attention and if one were honest, one had to admit that she seemed able to hold a light and amusing conversation with ease.

You didn't get passionate diatribes about conservation and global warming from her, but a cynical amusement at the vagaries of the world, which had even Megan chuckling several times, though she was annoyed at herself for that.

When the meal was over Nick excused himself. 'I still get a bit tired,' he said with an apologetic glance at his wife. 'I'd like to have an early night.'

It made Megan's blood boil to see displeasure showing so clearly on Cynthia's face. That woman had no sense of loyalty! Ben's expression, as usual in public, betrayed nothing.

Megan decided that she had had enough of this charade, more than enough. 'I'm tired, too. I've still not adjusted fully to the time change. Let's go up now as well, Ben.' She pushed her chair back without waiting for his answer and was relieved when he stood up, too.

Before he could speak, Cynthia said plaintively, 'But I'm not at all tired! Ben, why don't you stay and have just one more little drinkie with me? You don't look at all drowsy and I'll never get to sleep so early! You know what I'm like.'

Megan put her arm into Ben's and tugged.

He took a step away from the table. 'Sorry, Cynth. Another time, maybe.'

Nick stepped into the breach. 'You two go up. I'll just have one more drink with Cynthia. She forgets sometimes that you're newly-weds.'

Cynthia's face showed a momentary anger, then became smooth again.

Megan saw Nick watching his wife's reactions carefully. He does know, she realised suddenly. He knows exactly what she's like. Why doesn't he stop her tricks, then? And why did he marry her in the first place?

But Megan knew she had no right to be criticising anyone else's reasons for marrying. After all, she and her brand new husband hadn't got together for the usual reasons, either.

Ben's smile was replaced by a look of concern. 'You look as if you need a sleep more than we do, Nick.' He squeezed Megan's hand. 'Look, why don't we stay for one more drink? We'll let Nick get to bed while we tire this energetic woman out for him.'

There was nothing Megan could do but sit down again. Nick was indeed looking extremely weary and she didn't intend to allow Cynthia to have free access to Ben. Nor, it seemed, did he intend to make himself available to her. He sat down very close to Megan and put his arm round her shoulders, keeping it there.

Cynthia chatted brightly on through two more drinks to their one.

You had to give her credit for never being at a loss for a subject, thought Megan. But the warmth of Ben's arm was comforting and once she reached up to pat the hand that lay on her shoulder and smile at him.

As time passed, however, and the others showed no sign of moving, she yawned openly and nudged her husband.

He looked at her and nodded, then cut Cynthia off short. 'I really will have to tuck this wife of mine up in bed now, Cynth. It's been lovely bumping into you two. Tell Nick I'll see him on Monday to finalise those contracts.'

'Oh, it surely won't be that long till we meet again, us being in the same hotel. We're bound to bump into one another tomorrow.' Her words were slightly slurred. 'In fact, let's have dinner together again.'

You've had too much to drink, Megan thought. Not clever, Mrs Berevic.

'I'll just have another slurp or two,' Cynthia announced loudly and signalled to the waiter, but he didn't see her.

Megan was puzzled by the sudden tension in Ben's body. His hand dropped from her shoulder and he leaned forward. 'Don't you think you'd better join Nick now?' His words were a bit more than a suggestion.

Cynthia flapped a hand defiantly. 'Nope. Definitely not. He'll be asleep by now, anyway.' She waved at the waiter and this time he did see her and came over. 'I'll have another dry martini, please. A large one.'

Not only was her speech slightly slurred, but she was staring round at the other people sitting in the bar, eyes narrowed as if assessing them.

Ben sighed and closed his eyes for a minute. 'Look, you go up, Megan. I'll join you shortly.' He lowered his voice and added, 'I can't leave her when she's in this condition.'

Cynthia made no effort to conceal her jubilation.

Megan felt bitterly upset at Ben giving in to this blatant blackmail, but she wasn't going to give Cynthia the satisfaction of showing it. Making no attempt to say goodnight, she stood up and marched across the foyer, her back straight and her head held high.

Rage made her feet beat out a tattoo as she walked. It was only too obvious whose wishes were getting priority with her husband. Well, just let him lay one finger on her when he came back to their room--that was all! She'd pretend to be asleep.

If he came back to their room, said that little voice in her head, and she had to bite her lip to hold back the tears. She couldn't cope with much more of this, didn't see why she should have to, either. Ben wasn't playing fair by her - or by their agreement.

It was like being on a roller-coaster, and she'd never enjoyed those.

Chapter 10

The next morning Megan was shaken awake while it was still dark outside. She stared around, still feeling foggy-brained. 'What's wrong?'

'Wake up, sleepyhead!'

'What time is it?'

'Nearly six o'clock.' Ben switched on his bedside radio. 'We can listen to the news while we get ready. I want to be away before eight, if I can hire a car by then.'

She could only gape at him. 'Where are you going?' If he was going somewhere with Cynthia, whatever the excuse he made, that was it. She'd leave him!

She sat up in bed, studying his face in puzzlement. She'd meant to stay awake until he got back last night and confront him about Cynthia then, but she must have fallen asleep. Well, she always had trouble staying awake late and she was usually a very sound sleeper. Was he annoyed about that? No, his smile was a real one, the sort that curled your toes. She was smiling back before she knew it.

'It's not just me who's going somewhere,' he said. 'We are going away. As in together.'

She was fully awake now. 'Where? You never said anything yesterday.' What was going on here? Whatever it was, she liked it. Well, she thought she did.

'I made a sudden decision last night. I don't want to get trapped into another evening of drinking and keeping an eye on Cynthia. We're heading south this morning, milady. To our block of land. Do you or do you not want to see our magnificent country mansion?'

Relief surged through her - and pleasure, too. They'd be alone. No Cynthia. No business meetings. 'Well, of course I want to see it! Er - what time did you come up to bed last night?'

He pulled a wry face. 'Just after one o'clock. And that was only because the bar closed. You were sound asleep.'

'I'm sorry - I meant to wait up for you. That's why I left

the light on.'

He grinned. 'It had no effect. You seem to have a talent for falling asleep on me.'

Megan nodded, waiting for an explanation of why he had been so late, then, when it didn't come, telling herself she had to trust Ben. If she didn't, they'd stand no chance together. But it was hard sometimes. Very hard.

He was over by the wardrobe now, pulling things out and tossing them on to the bed.

'What's the hurry?'

He came over to the bed. 'You said you wanted to get away from luxury hotels, didn't you? Well, we're getting away. I want to leave before anyone starts ringing or sending me urgent messages. We'll come back on Monday morning. Well? Are you going to get up, or do I have to tip you out of bed?' He lifted one corner of the mattress, baring his teeth in a pirate's grin.

With a shriek, she abandoned her worries and leaped out of the other side of the bed, making for the bathroom. When she returned, wrapped in a towel, his suitcase was nearly full. As she dressed, she started calculating what to take, entering into the spirit of things, her spirits lifting by the minute. 'You order breakfast for me while I start my packing. Bacon and eggs will be fine. And maybe a few slices of toast. Oh, and a piece of fruit.'

He grimaced. 'I'll never understand how you can face that sort of thing so early in the morning.'

'Because I'm always hungry within half an hour of waking up. You'll just have to get used to it.'

When she was fully dressed, she hesitated in front of the mirror as she listened to him murmuring into the phone, arranging to pick up their hire car. Then, with a shrug, she simply bundled her hair into a pony tail and swept her make-up into a sponge bag without putting any on.

He blew her a kiss from as she came out of the bathroom and covered up the mouthpiece of the phone to whisper, 'Great! I like you best without make-up.'

'You look good without it, too.'

He chuckled, then went back to his conversation.

She looked at his one suitcase and the clothes still hanging in the wardrobe, and as he put the phone down, she asked, 'Aren't we taking the rest of our things with us?' They had brought considerable excess luggage on the plane, after the shopping in Singapore, and she had been horrified at how much that had cost. Since then, she had added a big pile of books to the number of things they had.

'Good heavens, no! We'll leave them here.'

'You mean you'll pay for the whole suite just to store our luggage?'

'Why not?' He shrugged.

'But that's a dreadful waste of money. It'll cost you a fortune.'

He looked at her in wonderment. 'You're the only female I've ever met in my whole life who's wanted to save me money, not spend it!' He gestured to their things. 'Anyway, what else can we do with all this? I don't want to clutter up the car I've hired, and we'll only have to bring the stuff back again.'

'We can see if the hotel has any storage space for guests or at the very least, we can hire their cheapest room to keep our things in.'

He threw out his arms in a gesture of submission and grinned. 'Very well, Scrooge. Whatever makes you happy.'

She beamed back at him. The real Ben was back again. At least, she thought this was the real Ben. And she hoped he'd stay, too, this time.

After picking up the hire car, a large, luxurious four-wheel drive, they headed south down the freeway. An hour later they arrived at Mandurah and he turned off the highway towards the town centre, which lay on the water. They took a brisk stroll along the foreshore to stretch their legs, following an attractive boardwalk along the water's edge.

'This is one of my favourite places in the whole world,' he said, waving at the people in a boat that was chugging slowly across the water.

She tried to hide her amazement. It was pretty enough, built along the sides of a very wide estuary, but surely he'd been to more striking places? Still, it was nice, she had to admit.

Several boats, large and small, were trailing across the water, cormorants were fishing and pelicans were coming in to land like miniature Boeing 747s. Suddenly she saw a fin and grabbed his arm. 'Is that what I think it is?'

'A dolphin.'

'Yes. Oh, and look, it's a mother and baby. I've never seen them in the wild before. It looks like it's attached to her by elastic.'

'They come up here often.' He grinned at her excitement and gave her a quick hug.

Although the morning was cool, the sun was shining and the sky was as blue as if it were summer. She breathed in the salty air and let it out in a long, happy sigh. 'This is absolutely marvellous, Ben!'

'Do you fancy a cup of coffee before we leave?'

'I'd love one. And a scone, perhaps?'

He rolled his eyes. 'Your appetite will be the ruin of me!'

'Well, you're rich enough to keep me in cake, aren't you?' It was the first time she'd felt truly comfortable joking about his wealth.

They sat outside a café near the waterfront at a white plastic table.

'What is a rich man like you doing in a place like this, Ben Saunders?' she asked, eyes dancing with amusement. 'Cheap plastic tables, no tablecloths!'

He laughed. 'Well, you did say you were tired of luxury hotels! And anyway, I'm getting hungry now.'

The food was good and the service cheerful. She watched Ben eat some currant toast with his coffee and then go on to demolish two freshly-baked scones, while she ate a huge piece of carrot cake.

'Remember Edinburgh,' he said softly, 'and the café there?'

'I felt such a fool, being carried like that.'

'You're no one's fool, Megan.'

It was nice to receive a compliment, but she would have rather had a 'Darling' or two. She swallowed hard on that longing and said brightly, 'What do we do about food for the rest of the day? And are there beds and bedding at this shack of yours?'

'A double bed and bedding, yes. Not much food, apart from a few tins. I usually drive somewhere and pick up a take-away. But,' he smiled and raked her body with his eyes, 'I might be too busy to do that, so I suppose we'd better go and buy some supplies. Are you a good cook?'

'Not bad. And you?'

'Terrible. I've never really had time to learn.'

'I'll have to teach you, then. It'd get boring being the only one doing the cooking.'

He blinked in obvious surprise. 'All right. You're on.'

She hid her amusement. If he wasn't liberated about sharing the chores now, he would be by the time they'd been together for a while. She didn't intend to turn into a resident housekeeper and general factotum like her friend Sandy.

When the car was loaded with unglamorous plastic shopping bags, Ben swooshed them off southwards again. After a few miles, he made a detour along a narrow road that ran round the edge of a huge expanse of water called the Peel Inlet.

'It's beautiful,' Megan said softly, as they stopped to watch some pelicans doing a well-choreographed slow-motion ballet by the water's edge.

'Just wait until summer. It doesn't rain for months. All the grass shrivels up and turns beige. That's when you have to watch out for bush fires.'

'In England, there would be buildings all the way around this lake, not to mention promenades and pleasure boats. Here there are only us and a few pelicans.' She threaded her arm through his.

'You get a lot more boats on the inlet in summer, though not many big ones. They run aground too easily. Most of that water is only about a metre and a half deep, except for the boating channels that have been dredged. In summer, you see people wading along a hundred yards from shore, towing a baby bath behind them into which they put the crabs they catch.'

'You're joking.'

'No, I'm not. Mandurah's famous for its crabs. Most people catch their own and then boil them up.'

'It sounds too good to be true.' For all the stern warnings she kept giving herself, happiness was fizzing inside her. 'Can we do that in the summer? Catch crabs, I mean?'

'Oh, yes.' He sat down on a wooden bench and leaned back. 'And we'll catch prawns, too. You go prawning after dark, boil them up over a camp fire, followed by a midnight feast.'

She sighed happily as she joined him on the bench. 'This is going to be heaven! Imagine still being able to do that.' She sat up abruptly. 'Are there still large stocks of prawns here?'

'Oh, yes. And of crabs. And bag limits on what you can catch.'

She relaxed again. 'Great. So I shan't feel guilty.'

After a moment or two of silence, he said abruptly, 'You're not really impressed by luxury or money, are you, Megan?'

She coloured a little. 'I've been spending your money, haven't I, using that credit card you gave me? Look at all the books I bought.'

'That's not real spending. Most of the women I know would be buying jewels and designer clothes.'

She felt embarrassed by the warmth of his gaze. 'Well, you've already bought me enough clothes to last for ages, and buying books is the sort of spending I like best. Do you have any bookshelves in your shack? If not, I'll splash out on some. And - and I'd like a computer, too, if that's all right. I had an old one in England, but it wasn't worth bringing it out here.'

'Why a computer?'

'Why not? They're fun.' She took a deep breath to give herself courage and added, 'I like going on the Internet and I'll want to keep in touch with my friends, particularly Sarah. And I, um, I write a little.' She held her breath, praying that he wouldn't mock her aspirations.

He nodded in instant comprehension. 'Ah! That's what you meant when you said you had some 'creative options' you could consider, isn't it?'

'Mmm.' Goodness, did he remember every word she had spoken?

'What do you write? Or do you prefer not to talk about it?'

She stared down at her toes. 'Short stories so far. I've had a couple published in women's magazines, actually. They even paid me for them. I - I want to try to write a novel next.'

There was silence, then he gave her a quick hug. 'You're full of surprises. Nice ones, too. And I'll be delighted to buy you a computer. I need a desktop for me as well. Laptops are great when you're travelling, but they're not comfortable to work on for long.'

He gave her one of his real smiles, the sort that turned him into every Prince Charming she had ever read about rolled into one, and she was beaming back at him before she knew it.

'You're looking happier today,' he murmured.

'I think I'm a country girl at heart. Do you mind?'

'On the contrary.'

He was humming as they set off. He had quite a nice voice, actually. She joined in, for the first time feeling relaxed enough to sing in front of him. She wasn't tone deaf or anything, but she didn't have a strong voice.

They arrived at the turn-off to his block of land some forty minutes later. It was a dirt track marked by a wooden letterbox on a pole with SAUNDERS painted on it. There was a rusty metal gate across the entrance which wouldn't keep intruders out for more than thirty seconds.

'I'll open it.' Megan jumped out of the car and swung on the gate like a child as it opened and closed, not minding that Ben was chuckling at her.

The track beyond was appalling, full of ruts and holes.

'The rain's washed away some of the gravel,' he said, frowning. 'I'd better have it graded by a bulldozer. I'm going to buy a four-wheel drive, I think, maybe one like this, not to mention a good, solid car for you. There are no buses out here in the bush. What sort of a car would you like?'

'Goodness, anything that goes will do me! Whatever they've got in the second-hand car yard.'

He gave her another of those strange looks. 'I'd rather you drove something with all the latest safety features, actually. And a car for you won't break the bank, believe me.'

It made her feel strange to hear him decide to buy something like two cars on the spur of the moment, especially on top of talking about getting them both desktop computers. No need to save up for anything. You just went out and got what you needed. Would she ever grow used to that?

She thought suddenly of the money she was expecting from the sale of her old car. Ben had laughed at her for even bothering about selling it.

Perhaps she could buy something for her aunt and uncle with it? Later. If things worked out for Ben and her. If she didn't need to keep a nest-egg, just in case. Oh, please, let them work out, she prayed desperately.

After a few hundred yards of rocking slowly along the rough track, they arrived at the house.

Megan stared at it in stunned silence. 'Is it . . . real?'

'What do you mean by that? Of course it's real.' He put on an injured expression, hand on heart. 'Don't you like my country mansion?'

They got out, each leaning on a car door. 'It looks like a child's playhouse,' she said at last. 'I mean, no builder would dare admit to putting up that thing, because he'd lose all his customers if he did. It's all bits and pieces stuck together with glue, and that tin roof's so rusty I bet it leaks.'

'I believe the original owner built the house himself. People used to do that quite often in Australia. This place is about eighty years old, ancient by local standards.'

'Is it safe?'

'Oh, yes. I had the electricity checked.' He pointed to a row of old wooden poles with wire strung along the tops that followed the line of the track. 'There isn't any phone line yet, though I'll have one run in now and get the electricity put underground at the same time. Oh, and there's no scheme water, either, but I had new water tanks installed and filled.'

'You mean - we don't have running water here?'

'Well, when you turn on the taps, water runs out of them, but if you run too much of it, you'll empty the tanks.'

They walked towards the house together and he stopped. 'Stay there a minute.' He crossed the tiny veranda in one stride and unlocked the front door, then, to her surprise, he swept her off her feet and carried her over the threshold.

She clung to him as he set her down, feeling tears start

in her eyes at this gesture.

He put his hands on her shoulders and looked at her face. 'You know, I think you're quite a romantic at heart.'

'I am.' She looked at him expectantly. Surely now he would say something a bit more loving? But he only smiled and took her hand.

'Right then, guided tour. This, Mrs Saunders, is your parlour. It's also your hallway, dining room, office and anything else that's not a bedroom.' He pulled her across to the other side of the room, where a rectangular alcove was built outwards from one wall to contain the kitchen, which had sagging old cupboards with peeling paint, but a new cooker and fridge.

'Good thing I never swing cats,' she joked, opening and shutting one of the cupboard doors, then peering into the huge fridge, empty except for a few cans of beer and lemonade. She switched on the fridge at the socket.

He took her hand again and led her across the main room, whose table, chairs and two sofas were not only new, but beautiful, the sort of furniture she would have chosen herself. She paused to stroke the wood. 'This is lovely.'

'I'm glad you like it.' Flinging open a door, he flourished a bow. 'Now this, madam, is the larger bedroom. It looks more like a cupboard, I know, but it does fit the bed in - just.'

'It's the same size as my aunt and uncle's bedroom,' she said quietly. 'Quite large enough for me, Ben.'

He squeezed her hand and nodded, as if he had expected that answer.

The other bedroom was even smaller and was unfurnished, with bare dusty boards and a sagging blind at the window. Megan could just picture it set up as an office, a place where she could write the stories that were seething inside her for expression.

She frowned as they went back into the main area. 'Um - isn't there a bathroom?' She didn't mind a humble home, but you could get a bit too primitive.

'The bathroom's outside.' He opened the door at the back of the main room to disclose another small veranda with what looked like a lean-to shed at one end. This proved to contain both a shower and laundering facilities of sorts.

Megan dissolved into giggles at the sight of the huge concrete laundry trough. 'Where's the stone?'

He looked puzzled.

'I'll need a stone to beat my washing with in that thing.'

He chuckled. 'I'll get you two stones. Much more efficient.'

'Isn't there a toilet?'

'Voilà!' He opened the door of what she had taken to be a cupboard and revealed a bright pink pedestal with a blue seat and cistern. She started laughing again, so much that she had to lean against him for support. 'Whoever chose that thing?'

'The owner, I presume. It's in working order, so I didn't like to disturb it for mere aesthetic reasons. But I thought we might paint the walls bright yellow and get some green toilet paper. That should really brighten up our quiet moments.'

By now, she was helpless with laughter and his deeper chuckles punctuated her gasps and splutters.

When they were back inside, waiting for the kettle to boil, she looked at him. 'Why did you think we'd need to rent a house, Ben?'

'I thought you might find this one too small, not to mention too primitive.'

'No. I think it's charming, or it could be. And just look at that view!'

'Won't you be bored so far away from everything?'

'I don't think so. What about you?' She realised she still didn't really know what he was like in everyday life, only what he was like in hotels, and that made her feel wistful. She didn't really know him very well at all in the ways that mattered long term. But they were getting closer all the time - in spite of Cynthia - in spite of business needs. They really were.

'I shan't be bored, Megan, I promise you. I'm a do-it-yourself addict when I have the time - even when I can afford to pay someone else.' He looked down at his hands and smiled. 'My grandfather would have been very scornful of a man with such soft hands.'

Then he looked up with an expression of happy anticipation. 'The roof here is still not quite watertight, the bathroom walls are sagging and there are a million other minor repairs needed. And besides that, I've got piles of house plans to look at.'

He saw her expression and corrected himself quickly. 'For us to look at, I mean. Um - I trained as an architect, actually, though I never practised. I have a few ideas about what sort of house I'd like to live in. I'd like to try designing it myself, if you don't mind.'

She was delighted that he was sharing his thoughts with her. 'That sounds fun. And what will you do here once the house is built? Won't you grow bored then?'

'No. I have one or two hobbies I haven't been able to indulge in for years. I might even take up golf. I'm really looking forward to having some free time, for once. Life has been gruelling for the last decade. It's you I'm worried about.'

She moved over to put her arms round his neck and lean her head on his shoulder. 'This house will be fine for me, Ben. And,' she leaned back and beamed at him suddenly, 'I'll really get to know the West Australian wildlife here. You're not going to cut down all that bush, are you?'

'Heavens, no! Especially now that I've married an eco-freak.'

'I'm no fanatic, just interested and wanting to do my bit.'

'Me, too - now that I've got time.'

As she made them a cup of coffee, she said thoughtfully, 'I would like to buy a few more bits and pieces for the house, though, simple things like cushions and good saucepans.'

'Go ahead. As soon as we get back to Perth you can shop till you drop.' He kissed her forehead, then the kettle began to boil and he moved away.

She went and sat down beside him on one of the lovely couches to drink her coffee, happier than she had been at any time since she'd met him.

The weekend passed in a daze of ongoing happiness for Megan. Ben had turned into a normal, fun-loving human being, instead of a business robot. Sometimes she had trouble believing he was the same person. Sometimes she had trouble believing she would not wake up and find herself dreaming. And just occasionally she even dared to hope he was growing more than merely fond of her. Not from what he said, but from the way he behaved, both in bed and out of it.

For most of their stay, the weather was kind to them and she was astonished that this was still winter. They walked all over the block. So much land and it all belonged to them. It was mostly uncleared, with the original bush plants still growing on it, many of them in flower, since it was winter.

Ben had already had a few paths bulldozed through the bush near the cottage because he didn't want anyone getting lost there. He taught her to recognise some of the native birds and plants, and she was thrilled one morning to wake up to a kookaburra shrieking with laughter outside the shack. That made her feel really Australian.

She planned to buy herself some more books on local wildlife and learn as much as she could. Perhaps they could set aside some land as a sort of animal sanctuary? And plant an arboretum on another part of the land?

'Whatever you like,' he said with a smile when she

broached those ideas. 'As long as you let me plant the trees for you. I love getting my hands dirty.'

'We'll both plant them - and watch them grow.'

Australia, she thought as she lay wakeful one night, was just as fascinating as she'd expected.

And Ben, in this mood, was Mr Perfect.

Except for the lack of endearments. It was silly to care so much about that, but she did.

Once or twice she walked quietly down to the water on her own, to sit on a fallen tree trunk and soak up the peace as she watched the birds wheeling and circling over the water of the inlet.

Ben didn't follow her. He seemed to understand her need for time to herself and to have a similar need to be on his own now and then.

On the Sunday afternoon, the sound of rain on the tin roof delighted her, pattering softly as they went to bed, rather like a lullaby.

Later on, it woke them both up, pounding heavily on the roof, but she wouldn't admit that it was too noisy.

'Damn! I can hear water dripping,' Ben said suddenly.

'You must have excellent hearing.'

'Yes. I do. But I'll have to get up and put a bucket under the leak.'

He had to get up twice more, as well.

'Repairing that roof is going to be my first priority,' he said when he came back to bed.

On the Monday morning she woke first, to lie staring at him, apprehension whispering inside her. It was time to return to Perth. Time for the businessman to re-emerge. Time to face Cynthia again. And she was, Megan admitted to herself, terrified of losing the fragile rapport she was building with her husband.

Ben woke and smiled at her sleepily. 'Let's stay here.'

'I wish we could.'

'So do I. But we'll come back soon.'

He kept up a light banter as he drove them north towards Perth, but Megan could feel herself growing gradually quieter.

She was dreading meeting Cynthia again, even if this was just going to be a brief encounter as Ben and Nick finalised their mutual business arrangements.

Most of all, she was dreading losing this feeling of closeness to her husband.

Chapter 11

Returning to Perth was like returning to prison after the open freedom of the countryside. Megan could feel herself getting edgy within minutes of hitting the city traffic and she noticed that Ben had lost his relaxed air.

'We could go and look at cars before we go back to the hotel,' he said as they approached the city centre. 'Not too tired, are you?'

'No, of course not.'

They examined dozens of vehicles and eventually they, or rather Ben, chose two, a dark blue four-wheel drive vehicle for him and a white station wagon for her.

Just like that, she thought in amazement as they drove to the hotel. Buy two new cars as if they were grocery items. She could remember how hard she'd had to save for her first and only car.

I'll never let myself get blasé about such things, she vowed. Never. Nor will I waste money, just because I can afford to.

An urgent message from Cynthia was waiting for them at the hotel. As Megan watched Ben read it, his expression grew grim and her instincts told her it would take him away from her. She was right.

'Nick's in hospital,' he said curtly, in answer to her questioning look. 'I'll have to go and see him.'

'Has he had another heart attack?'

'Cynthia doesn't say, exactly.'

'Do you want me to come with you?'

'No. I'd rather see how ill he is first. He'll talk more freely if it's just me.' Almost as an afterthought, he added, 'Will you be all right?'

'Of course I will. Don't worry about me. I'll unpack and start on the shopping list for the house.'

A ghost of a smile crossed his face. 'You won't run off and go cruising down the river without me? You will be here when I return?'

'I'll be here unless you keep me waiting too long. In which case, I'll be down in the coffee shop having something to eat. How long do you think you'll be?'

'Shouldn't be more than an hour.'

She unpacked, made her first shopping list for the house, then curled up on the bed with one of the novels she had bought. But she couldn't settle to reading and found she was missing Ben's company more than she'd expected.

As two hours turned into four, she went down for a snack, then returned. She tried watching TV, but couldn't find anything that interested her. Where was Ben? Why hadn't he got in touch? It shouldn't have taken him this long to visit the hospital. And anyway, even though he hadn't got her a mobile phone yet, he could have called her via the hotel.

At six-thirty she had a shower and changed for dinner, not wanting to eat alone in their suite. She scribbled a note and was just about to go down to the restaurant when Ben returned.

He came across and gave her a perfunctory peck on the cheek. 'I'm sorry, Megan. Everything took much longer than I'd expected. I had to help Nick with some business as well as attend to my own.'

'You might have rung and let me know.'

'It wasn't convenient to leave the discussions. I've said I'm sorry.' His tone was sharper than usual.

'What exactly have you been doing for Nick?'

'Cynthia and I had to look at some property he was negotiating for, so that I could take over the negotiations, then I had to discuss prices and terms with the vendors. Nick will lose the whole deal if it isn't sewn up quickly, and it's rather a big one, so I've agreed to take it on board.' He glanced at his watch. 'Look, I'll just take a quick shower and change, hmm? I feel grubby.'

She watched him vanish into the bathroom. He had his leave-me-alone-I'm-busy look again. How she hated it when he shut her out!

And he'd been with Cynthia. She hated that, too.

He put his head round the bathroom door. 'Could you get my navy suit out, please? And a shirt and tie? We have to go to a business dinner with Cynthia, I'm afraid. What you're wearing will be fine.'

Heart sinking, Megan did as he asked and then sat watching as he dressed. He had scarcely looked at her. She could have been ninety years old and dressed in a sack for all he seemed to have noticed, and she was wearing a very flattering dress and had taken great care with her hair. How could he change so quickly?

When they all met, it seemed to her that for a woman whose husband was in hospital, Cynthia was in fine fettle.

The evening passed slowly. The other men were pleasant enough and had brought their wives along, but after the meal, the women gathered around one end of the table and left the men to talk business at the other end.

The other women discussed clothes and followed that by a lively debate on the attractions of various jewels, not so much concerned with their beauty, as with which were more likely to increase in value.

Megan was driven nearly to screaming point by it all and when pressed for her opinion on jewels said curtly that she preferred a good book, which made them all stare at her as if she had two heads. Then, when the topic changed to fur coats and they asked her which fur she preferred she said bluntly that many of those skins came from endangered species, and she was surprised they were still even considering wearing them.

'Oh, that eco-stuff is old hat now,' one woman said languidly. 'And about time, too. There's nothing as beautiful as fur and people are using it as a fashion statement again.'

'It's especially beautiful when it's on a live creature's back,' Megan snapped.

That got her a few more funny looks, but she didn't care. From down the table Ben shook his head at her, as if warning her not to pursue this point. She snapped her lips shut, breathing slowly and evenly, ignoring the next fascinating discussion about which designer labels were more 'in' at the moment.

Cynthia was included in the men's discussion, but that sounded equally boring to Megan. One man went on and on about property development and the iniquities of local government regulations. He seemed to be more interested in getting round the rules, than in building safely. Ben didn't contribute much at all to the conversation, just smiled slightly and nodded from time to time.

The final straw came when the party broke up and Cynthia claimed Ben's arm on the grounds that she was just a trifle tiddly. She was, thought Megan grimly, watching the other woman wobble towards a taxi, more than a trifle tiddly; she was downright drunk.

At the hotel, Ben took Cynthia to her hotel room while Megan went back to their suite on her own, feeling angry and abandoned.

He wasn't long in rejoining her. 'Goodness!' she said sourly as he came in. 'I'd expected you to stay for another nightcap or two with dear Cynthia.'

'Could we drop the sarcasm and just get to bed? I'm exhausted.' For once, he made no attempt to make love to her, just sighed and lay down, one arm across his eyes.

'Is the business finished now?' she asked, feeling a bit guilty for her sharpness when she realised how tired he looked.

'Mine is. Nick's needs a little more attention.' He roused himself to look at her and say, 'It always tires me out, negotiating, don't know why. Perhaps because you have to be hyper-alert the whole time, if you want to win.' He sighed and rubbed his forehead, then closed his eyes again.

She hadn't realised that. He didn't often confide in her. 'How is Nick? Better?'

'Mmm.'

Deep, even breathing told her that he was asleep. She

switched off the light and hunched herself into a ball of misery. She had missed him today more than she would have believed possible before their visit to the house. And although he didn't use endearments, he usually cuddled her before they went to sleep, even if they weren't making love.

It was a while before she managed to get to asleep. She told herself she was a fool to be jealous of his work, but that didn't make any difference to how she felt.

Was it always so hard being in love with someone?

Or was it only when that person didn't love you in return?

In the morning, Ben jerked out of a heavy sleep, looking strained even before he began and Megan felt guilty about her own resentment of the previous evening. After gulping down a cup of black coffee, he looked at the time. 'I'm afraid I'll be gone all day again. Will you be all right?'

'I'll be fine. I have plenty of shopping to do, after all.' Megan could not keep the edge from her voice, but she refrained from asking if dear Cynthia would be spending the day with him.

He looked at her then at his watch again and shook his head. 'I'm sorry. I really am, but I must go.'

At the door he turned. 'Look, would you buy yourself a mobile phone - and could you visit Nick this afternoon? Tell him everything's going really well with the deal. We don't want him worrying about anything?'

'Yes, I'll do that. Is it really going well?'

'It's touch and go at the moment, I'm afraid.' He hesitated, blew her a kiss from the door and then hurried away.

His remark made Megan feel guilty about her own sharp words. Clearly he had a heavy burden on his shoulders. Though why Cynthia couldn't visit her own husband was more than she would ever understand. If Ben had been in hospital she'd have been camped outside his room.

But then, she was stupid like that.

In a sudden fit of annoyance at the whole situation, including herself, she picked up a fat, self-satisfied cushion from the fat, self-satisfied sofa and hurled it at the door.

That made her feel slightly better. But only slightly.

She felt left out. Uncertain. Marking time.

When she visited the hospital later, she thought Nick looked grey and tired.

'I'm turning into an old crock,' he said apologetically.

No need to take out her ill humour on him. 'Oh, we all have our bad patches. You'll get better gradually.'

'I've spoiled your honeymoon, too.'

'No, you haven't.' She launched into a sprightly description of their days in Singapore, then went on to describe the block and the tiny wooden house. That soon had him laughing.

'I'm glad Ben married you,' he said unexpectedly. 'You'll be good for him.'

'Oh. Well, thank you.' She could feel herself blushing. 'I hope so.'

'Tell Cynth not to bother visiting me tonight,' he called as she left. 'She'll be tired after the day's meetings.'

From which Megan deduced that Cynthia was spending the day with Ben again. Why had he not told her that himself?

She went off to buy a mobile phone, choosing a case for it out covered in glittery beads.

Two long days followed, during which Megan explored the town and purchased some things for the house. She tried not to worry about exactly what Cynthia and Ben were doing, but couldn't help wondering. And she had to endure the other woman's company over dinner each evening until quite a late hour.

She had decided to stay up with them, however long it took. She wasn't giving Cynthia free access to Ben. They had to escort the stupid woman to her room, because each evening their glamorous companion drank a great deal, and although she held her liquor well, she did start flirting with any and every man when she'd sunk a few of her favourite dry martinis.

On the afternoon of their third day back in Perth, Ben came back to their hotel room looking triumphant. 'It's done! Signed, sealed and delivered. And I did rather well for Nick, if I say so myself.'

He grabbed Megan and waltzed her round the room. 'That, my fine lady, is the last of these business deals. My herculean toils are done. My life is now my own.'

She brightened up. 'Does that mean we can go home?'

'Home? Do you really think of that little shack as home?'

She nodded.

He smiled at her. 'You're an incredible woman.'

She could feel herself blushing and said hastily, 'So - can we go home now?'

'Well . . . ' His smile faded and he hesitated.

'Now what?' She could hear the edge to her voice, but couldn't help it.

'The hospital wants to run a series of tests on Nick. I don't like to leave Cynthia here on her own.'

Megan pulled out of his arms. 'What are you going to do, then, invite her to join us in this suite?' She gestured to the bed. 'It'll fit three, if we're all very friendly!'

He was avoiding her eyes. 'I've, um, invited her to come down to the block with us.'

'Cynthia?'

'Why not?' But he sounded defensive.

Megan gave a scornful laugh. 'She'll be bored out of her tiny! She's the last person to enjoy a place like that.'

'She says she enjoys an occasional visit to the country.'

'I'll bet she does.' Megan breathed deeply for a moment or two to prevent herself from saying something she might regret. She simply couldn't understand what Cynthia was after. 'Just a small point, though - where is she going to sleep?'

'We have a spare bedroom.'

'It's microbe-sized and unfurnished.'

'I'll have some furniture delivered. A single bed and a wardrobe should do it. I'll ring a shop up in Mandurah or Bunbury.'

'Better add a dressing table for her make-up. She even wears lipstick to breakfast. We wouldn't want to subject her to the hardship of putting it on with a hand mirror, would we?'

His lips tightened, but he only said, 'Very well.'

'Ben - '

'Yes?'

'Oh, Ben, I don't want that woman at our house! She'll spoil things.'

He scowled at her. 'You're being very childish. She won't be an easy guest, I agree, but Nick's worrying about her and that's not good for him. I'm doing this for him, not for her.'

' You didn't even think to ask me, though! Don't I have any say about who comes to stay in my home?' She knew even as she said it she was being unfair, but she was so disappointed, she couldn't help it. She didn't want that woman spoiling their little paradise.

The quarrel lasted barely five minutes, but it proved that Ben hadn't forgotten how to lose his temper and that Megan's tongue had retained its bite.

In the end, he stormed over to the door. 'I'm going downstairs for a drink and a bit of peace. You can stay here and sulk on your own. No one in his right mind would want to spend time with someone in such a shrewish mood!'

Megan sank down on the couch, but her fury gradually turned into embarrassment at the things she had said about Cynthia. Temper and yes, jealousy, had made her behave like a spoilt brat, no dignity, just what he had said - a shrew.

It was bad tactics, too, no way to keep him out of that woman's clutches. That was much more important.

Only you shouldn't need to consider tactics when speaking to your own husband.

She dashed away a tear. She would not cry! Another tear followed, so she blew her nose vigorously and began to walk round the room, breathing in and out very loudly, and stopping a couple of time to pummel the cushions on the couch. Very satisfying, that.

'Oh, hell, I suppose I'll have to apologise,' she said aloud after a while. She couldn't fool herself that she had behaved anything but abominably.

'He shouldn't have invited her, but I shouldn't have spoken like that, shouldn't have accused him of flaunting his mistress in front of my nose. Even if he is. Which he isn't. At least, I don't think he is.'

But she wasn't even sure of that; she was just sure she didn't want to do anything else that might alienate him, especially now. At the block, she had felt they were really starting to get close, then the minute they returned to Perth, he'd changed abruptly.

Even if what he was doing was stressful, he shouldn't shut her out like that. And she didn't enjoy living with a Jekyll and Hyde of a husband. She needed stability, certainty. She had done ever since her parents died, perhaps more than other people did. She acknowledged that.

But what did he need emotionally?

Anything at all?

The telephone rang. She sat staring at it, and only when it had rung five times did she reach out and pick it up. 'Hello?' Even in her own ears, her voice sounded sulky.

'Ben here. Darling, I've just bumped into Cynthia in the lobby. Why don't you come down and join us for drinks? Please, Megan!'

Bitterness flooded through her. The first time he had ever called her 'Darling' and it was, quite clearly, for that woman's benefit. She opened her mouth to say no, then she heard Cynthia's drawling voice in the background and took a deep breath instead. She wasn't going to let that sneaky bitch walk away with her husband! No way. 'How delightful of you to think of me!' she said coolly. 'I'll be about ten minutes. I haven't changed yet.'

'Thanks, love. I know you're tired and we'd agreed to eat in our room, but Cynthia was on her own.'

So that was the excuse he'd made? Megan smiled, albeit a bit grimly, but hope twitched again in her heart. He'd called to her for help. He hadn't just gone off with Cynthia.

She put the phone down and stared at it. Best of all, he had sounded really relieved when she agreed to join them. 'Oh, damn!' she said aloud. 'I don't know what to think any more!'

She kicked a stray cushion out of her way and dived for the wardrobe, choosing a sexy little black dress that had rather embarrassed her when Ben chose it in Singapore. She left her hair loose in a cloud and contented herself with the merest lick of make-up, but sprayed herself liberally with his favourite perfume.

She was unaware of how magnificent she looked, with her eyes still sparkling with anger and her cheeks softly flushed, but Ben noticed at least three men turn to watch her as she walked across the foyer to join them.

He also noticed the annoyance on Cynthia's face as Megan leaned across to kiss his cheek and whisper something in his ear, before pulling up a chair as close to him as she could get and saying casually, 'Hi, Cynthia!'

The meal was studded with innuendo, spiced with malice, but Megan gave as good as she got. Ben watched her in both admiration and amusement. Later, when she began making noises about it being late, he stood up immediately and they left Cynthia sitting sulking on her own in the foyer bar.

'Don't forget we're making an early start,' he called back over his shoulder.

Well, thought Megan, triumphantly as they walked across the foyer, that went better than I'd expected. I hope

Cynthia is so tiddly that she falls over when she tries to go up to her own room, and is too ill to come with us tomorrow. This image made her feel quite cheerful.

'Thanks for coming down,' Ben said as they got ready for bed.

'You sounded a bit desperate when you phoned.'

'I was. I really didn't fancy a tête-à-tête with Cynthia. Not after a long, tiring day in her company.'

In the darkness Megan smiled. Things were looking up. When he reached for her, she turned to him happily, revelling in his masculine hardness, his oh-so-clever fingers and soon riding with him down a white water trail of sheer ecstasy.

'It doesn't come much better than that,' he gasped afterwards.

But somehow, that remark spoiled her mood. Skilful techniques were no substitute for tenderness, well, not in her book. And the fact that he'd called her 'Darling' only for Cynthia's benefit still rankled.

The following morning, Megan woke to the realisation that she was about to spend a few days in close contact with Cynthia. For once she didn't feel like her normal, cheerful morning self. She scowled at Ben across the breakfast table and when they were getting ready to leave for the block in Ben's new Land Cruiser, she could hardly bring herself to be civil to him.

'I'll go and see if Cynthia is ready,' he said stiffly.

Megan grunted. She did not dare answer that remark or she'd have said something she might regret.

When he came back, he was looking even more tight-lipped. 'We'll have to get the other car and drive both of them down. Cynthia has rather a lot of luggage and there's all the new stuff you bought for the house as well. I'll go up and phone from our room. You might as well grab a coffee while we wait for it.'

There followed an hour's delay while the other car was

hastily delivered by the dealer and the luggage redistributed. Cynthia, of course, was riding with Ben.

'I'm sorry about this,' he whispered to Megan as they put things into the boot of her car.

'Not as much as I am!' She walked round to the driving seat and made herself comfortable.

Ben came across to hover beside the driver's window. 'Are you sure you'll be all right driving on your own?'

'Of course I will! I bought a little booklet and I know the road rules off by heart now,' she said brightly, aware that Cynthia was standing listening to every word, a smug smile on her face. As Megan started the motor, she watched resentfully as Ben helped Cynthia into the Land Cruiser.

'I'll be just fine!' she said aloud, but her hands were trembling as she put the car into drive and eased off the hand brake. She wasn't going to let that woman find out how nervous she felt about driving in Australia for the first time.

The morning rush was long past, so the journey down the freeway was quite peaceful and Megan's confidence grew quickly. This wasn't all that different from driving in England. She didn't know why she'd been worrying.

By the time they arrived in Mandurah, she was actually enjoying herself and would have been content to grab a quick sandwich, but Cynthia insisted she was starving, so they had lunch in a large hotel built round an indoor swimming pool.

'We should have gone to that café we found last time,' Megan said, keeping her expression wide-eyed and innocent. 'The food was delicious and the decor most original. Such lovely expensive furniture.'

Ben choked on his orange juice. 'Er - not quite Cynthia's style.' They exchanged amused glances and the tension between them eased a little.

'We'd better get some groceries,' she said.

'Yes. Coming, Cynthia?'

'I'll wait here. You can come back for me.'

Megan cheered up some more at the sight of Ben's annoyed expression

When they went to pick her up, she'd gone missing. Ben found her in the bar and his face grew even grimmer.

That pleased Megan.

When they arrived at the entrance to their block, Megan enjoyed watching Cynthia get out of Ben's car with a sulky expression on her face and totter along in her high heels to open the rusty gate.

But there was no pleasure in allowing that woman on to their private territory. In fact, it felt as if they were bringing Plague Mary home with them.

Megan watched as Cynthia gulped audibly at the sight of the tiny shack and looked around to check that this was really it. Grinning, she led the way inside. 'Welcome to our bijou country residence.'

The small bedroom was still unfurnished, so Cynthia couldn't unpack, but the shop had promised to deliver the bed and other things that afternoon.

How about a walk down to the water?' Megan asked once they had unloaded everything. 'We'll be able to hear anyone coming to deliver the bed if we don't go too far.'

Cynthia yawned. 'I'd much rather have a nice little G and T and put my feet up.'

'Oh, sorry!' said Megan briskly. 'We forgot to buy any gin. In fact, I don't think we have any alcohol here at all apart from a couple of cans of beer and one bottle of white wine.'

Ben looked sideways at her, as if he perfectly well understood that she had done that on purpose, and she found it hard to keep her face straight. So did he and they both had to look away from one another or they'd have burst out laughing.

'Let's go for that walk, then,' Ben suggested.

Cynthia ignored that offer and glared at her hostess. 'Well, I'll just have to go out and buy us all something to drink, won't I? My contribution to the weekend. I'll leave you two country cousins to go walkabout here. Lend me your car keys, Ben.'

He hesitated, then handed the keys over.

'Which way do I turn outside the gates?'

'Right. You might as well go into Bunbury, which is closer. Sure you can find your way back?'

'Oh, yes. Quite sure.'

Once Cynthia had gone, the quietness wrapped them round and they both let out long sighs of relief. Ben came and put his arms round Megan, standing holding her close. 'I hope she takes all afternoon.'

'So do I!' In fact, Megan couldn't understand why Cynthia had come with them at all, but it wouldn't be wise to say so. 'What did you do with your new mobile phone? Mine's not working properly, I'm afraid.'

'Oh, hell! I left mine in our room when I was talking to the car yard. Why? Do you need something?'

'I was just hoping Cynthia would get tired and want to go back to Perth. We could have phoned for a limousine to take her there in style. I wouldn't complain at all about the extravagance of that.'

They looked at one another and burst out laughing. As before, the block was working its magic on them.

But would that continue once Cynthia returned?

Megan found that she had underestimated Cynthia's sticking power. When the latter returned at dusk, the Land Cruiser was loaded with booze and parcels. Cynthia emerged from it wearing a new outfit - pale blue jeans and designer sneakers.

'I've been into Bunbury,' she announced. 'There aren't any good shops there, but I did manage to find a few things I needed. Do you like my country gear?' She paraded in front of Ben, her breasts thrusting against the sweater and her bottom undulating.

'You look lovely, as always.' But his glance didn't linger

on her.

'Dark blue or black jeans might have been more practical,' Megan said. 'Those will show the dirt.'

Cynthia pouted. 'Oh, practical! Who cares about that? Anyway, I've bought several pairs, so it won't matter. I can have them laundered when we get back.' She draped herself over the couch. 'Make me a martini, will you, Ben? The booze is in that box you just carried in. Shopping's made me thirsty.'

With great reluctance, Megan pulled out one of her brand new highball glasses and plonked it down in front of her husband.

'Now, darlings, did my bed arrive, or am I sleeping on the floor?' From the glitter in Cynthia's eyes, Megan was beginning to wonder if she had had a drink or two while she was out.

'Yes, it arrived. I've made it up for you.'

'Such a gracious hostess!' Cynthia murmured softly, one eye on Ben. 'I know exactly how pleased you are to have me here, Megan.'

She decided on equal frankness. 'Why the hell did you come, then?'

'I thought it might be interesting. Such fun to see you squirm. You won't keep him, you know. You're just a novelty. A man like that prefers sophisticated women.' She raised her voice, 'Ah, thank you, Ben! You always remember exactly how I like it.' Her voice was husky with other meanings.

Megan got up, sickened to see that woman blatantly flirting with her husband in her own home and itching to respond. 'I need a cup of coffee. What about you, Ben?'

'That'd be lovely.'

Megan had too much pride to burn the steaks, or produce anything except a perfect salad, but she couldn't help fantasising about making a dressing of arsenic or ground glass for Cynthia as she shredded the lettuce and tried to listen to what the other two were discussing. And she kept wondering how they would keep up even this superficial politeness for several days.

Well, Ben might manage it, but she'd find it extremely difficult.

No, impossible.

During the next two days, Megan felt her rapport with her husband slipping and couldn't work out how to remedy that. Their guest, she decided grimly, could out-act her any day - and did so regularly.

Cynthia, having decided to 'go country', as she phrased it, made no complaints about short walks in the bush, or bird-watching by the water, though she did seek alcoholic refreshment at regular intervals. She phoned the hospital to check on Nick's progress the next afternoon and spoke to him briefly.

On the second day, she discovered that the battery of her mobile was flat and she'd forgotten her charger. Thereafter, she insisted on Ben driving her along to the nearest phone morning and afternoon, to check that 'poor dear Nick' was all right.

'Why don't you drive yourself?' Megan asked bluntly.

'I'm worried the news might be bad. And then I'd be too upset to drive. Besides, I enjoy the company.' She smiled smugly.

If Cynthia really thought that there was a chance of Nick getting worse, Megan fumed as she waited for them to return, then she should have stayed up in Perth near him.

Going to bed was no relief, either, because Megan was so tense she couldn't enjoy making love. The mere thought of Cynthia overhearing them gave her the shudders and took all the pleasure out of it.

'Can't you relax a little,' he murmured in her ear the first night.

'Not with her in the house! She might hear us.' The bed next door creaked and she added, 'In fact, she'd definitely hear us.'

'For goodness' sake, she's not a monster, just a rather foolish woman who needs company. I'll switch the radio on when we make love.'

'You will not! She'll know exactly why we've done that.'

'Who cares?'

'I do!'

He sighed and turned over. 'Then we'll leave it for tonight. I'm not into necrophilia.'

Which didn't make Megan feel any better. 'What is that woman, a child who needs baby-sitting?'

'In some ways, yes.'

She turned her back to him. 'Well, I've no desire to be her baby-sitter, thank you very much!'

'I'm under considerable obligation to Nick.'

'Well, you baby-sit her, then! Take her out somewhere tomorrow and give me a bit of peace!'

'I'd rather you came with us.'

'I'd rather not spend any more time with her than I have to! She's driving me crazy!'

Even a game of Scrabble the previous evening had been filled with sexual innuendoes from Cynthia. But Megan had won.

For what that was worth.

The following morning, Ben suggested they all drive down to Busselton, where there was apparently a long jetty which you could ride along in a little train and watch the fish swimming in the water beneath you.

'No thanks! You two go.' Megan began to wash the dishes. 'But you can bring back some steaks for tea. We'll have a barbecue.' She glanced out of the window. 'If it stays fine.'

Cynthia purred her approval and was ready to leave in record time, her blond hair gleaming softly behind a white bandeau.

Ben scowled at Megan, pausing at the door to ask, 'Are you sure you won't change your mind and come with us?'

'I'm certain. You're welcome to dance attendance on dear Cynthia. I'll have a nice restful day. Don't forget to take some booze with you. She probably won't last until you get to Busselton without a tipple or two.'

'Keep your voice down. She'll hear you.'

'I don't care if she does.'

He moved towards the door. 'You've been nothing but bad-tempered since we came down here and I'm getting tired of it. Quite frankly, I'll be glad to spend a day with someone who isn't sulking.'

'That's fine by me!'

But it wasn't fine by her. When they had left, she threw herself on the bed and sobbed, then got mad at herself for being so spineless. She stood up, blew her nose several times and went to clean the kitchen, attacking it as if it were her personal enemy.

Afterwards, she went out for a walk, taking her new Australian bird book with her. But she couldn't concentrate on it, couldn't concentrate on anything but her own worries about her marriage.

When she was a long way from the house, it started to rain. She had been too preoccupied to study the sky, so it took her completely by surprise.

'That's all I needed!' she shrieked at the grey clouds.

The rain pelted down even harder and she stuffed the book under her top.

By the time she got back, she was soaked through and her legs were plastered with mud. 'Fine sunny country this is!' she grumbled as she peeled off her soggy clothing and left it in the laundry trough. 'It does nothing but rain.'

A lukewarm shower did not help much and she still felt chilled as she piled on some clothes afterwards.

As she huddled on the couch, she decided she had been utterly stupid to play into Cynthia's hands by leaving her alone with Ben. She wished she had gone with them, wished she didn't love him, because it made her so vulnerable, wished she had never married him - No! She shook her head. She didn't wish that, would not undo it even if she could. 'You're a fool, though!' she told herself.

'I know I am,' she sighed a moment later. 'But I can't seem to help myself where he's concerned.'

She went back into the laundry to wash her clothes. It felt so cold out there she left them soaking. There was no hot water left, anyway.

It was chilly inside the house, too, because she'd forgotten to stoke up the ancient pot-bellied stove which also heated the water. The old fire was rather awkward and she hadn't really got the hang of it yet. If they were going to live here, they'd have to get a better heater for the house, and an electric heater for the water.

It had been paradise when there were just the two of them. Now it was more like purgatory. And a damp, chilly purgatory, too.

She sneezed and shivered as she struggled with the last of their newspaper and tried to light a fire with the damp wood. Was she catching a cold? That'd be the final straw. Fancy trying to compete against Cynthia's elegance with a red nose!

She couldn't concentrate on the book. And when she went over to turn up the fire, she found it had gone out again. But she wouldn't let herself cry. Well, only a stray tear or two.

Chapter 12

By the time Ben and Cynthia returned, the rain was falling steadily and the roof had started to leak, not a gentle drip this time, but a steady trickle. Megan had emptied the bucket several times, braving the icy wind that seemed to be scouring the warmth from the landscape. She contemplated another attempt to light that fire, but couldn't be bothered.

In fact, her body felt at as low an ebb as her spirits. Perhaps she had been wrong to marry Ben? He didn't love her and never would. Why should he? She was so ordinary, compared with the women he had associated with before.

When she heard the car drive up, she didn't make any attempt to go outside. As the front door opened she greeted them with, 'The roof's leaking worse than ever.'

Cynthia stared at the drip bucket as if she had never seen such a thing before. 'How quaint!'

Ben, whose mood seemed to match Megan's, came over to scowl at the water filling the bucket rapidly and growled, 'That's all I need!'

He didn't look at her, let alone kiss her or touch her. She had clearly driven him away.

But then she realised he wasn't looking at Cynthia, either. Indeed, the two of them were looking everywhere but at each other. A tiny seed of curiosity and hope began to draw Megan out of her misery.

In fact, they looked like people who had been quarrelling. Had he not enjoyed his day out, then? Oh, she hoped not!

Cynthia went to leave her handbag in the bedroom and came back smelling strongly of perfume to drape herself along the other couch. 'Any chance of a cup of coffee, Megan?'

'You're more than welcome to make some!' She sneezed several times in rapid succession. Her eyes were watering and she was sure her nose was red. He'd think she looked like a clown. Well, she probably did.

Ben came across the room and stared down at her. 'Are you all right?'

'Just a bit cold. I went out for a walk and got soaked.' Another shiver ran through her. 'I haven't been able to get warm since. I tried to light that stupid stove, but the wood's all wet and we didn't have any more newspapers.'

She couldn't prevent her voice from shaking and tears welling in her eyes. If Cynthia hadn't been there, she'd have flung herself into Ben's arms and howled all over his chest, just for the pleasure of being held and comforted. As it was, she could only sniff and try to blink the tears away.

He patted her arm. 'I've got a couple of newspapers in the car. You stay there and I'll soon have a fire started, wet wood or not.'

Megan leaned her head back, closing her eyes to blot out the vision of blond elegance opposite her. Cynthia made no attempt to get any coffee. When Ben returned, a gust of cold damp air blew in.

'You'll have to empty the bucket!' he said sharply.

Megan opened her eyes, unable to believe that he was speaking so harshly after telling her to rest.

'Not you, Megan. Cynthia.'

Their guest sat bolt upright. 'Me? Empty that rusty old thing!'

'It's not all that heavy,' he said briskly. 'Shove the plastic bucket underneath the drip and empty that one. I'm busy with the fire and poor Megan is chilled through.'

When Cynthia didn't move, he added more sharply, 'The bucket's nearly overflowing. Go and chuck the water off the edge of the back veranda, then make us all a cup of coffee.'

He went into the bedroom, returning with a blanket, which he draped over his wife. 'You're to stay there until you're warm again, and no arguing!'

She nodded, touched by his concern. As she looked up, she met his eyes and warmth flooded through her. That might not be love in his expression, but it was certainly affection. Which wasn't to be scorned.

The blanket seemed a tangible proof that he cared about her. She snuggled into it, smiling as she listened to Cynthia grumbling about the weight of the bucket, nearly choking with suppressed laughter as she watched the other woman walking awkwardly to avoid splashing her jeans.

When Megan's eyes met Ben's, she had to bite on her index finger to prevent herself from chuckling aloud. Suddenly she felt much better.

He came across and bent over to kiss her lightly on the cheek, whispering, 'I'll take her back to Perth tomorrow, I promise. Come with me? Please don't leave me alone with her again. Ever.'

A shriek of outrage from outside made them both jerk up in shock.

'What the - ' Ben began.

Cynthia came running in, brushing muddy water off herself, and slammed the dripping bucket down on the floor. 'I'm not emptying that filthy thing again!'

Ben's face remained expressionless, but Megan had to blow her nose hard.

'Just look at me!' Cynthia shrieked, waving her hands at him. 'I'm soaked! Absolutely soaked. And it's rusty water. It'll never come off! My new jeans are ruined!'

'What happened?' he asked, all wide-eyed innocence.

She began to dab at herself with the tea towel. 'The dirty water blew back at me, that's what happened!'

'Oh yes. I should have warned you to check the wind direction first. Never mind, you'll soon dry out and you'll know better next time, won't you?'

'Next time! If you think, Ben Saunders, that I'm going to even touch that damned bucket again, you've got rocks in your head!'

Megan had to change another laugh into a strangled cough.

Ben said blandly, 'You shouldn't let these little things upset you, Cynthia. What you need, what we all need, is a hot drink. Why don't you put the kettle on?'

She glared at his back, but he had bent once more over the recalcitrant fire and wasn't paying her any attention.

Megan concentrated on repeating the twelve times table inside her head, to stop herself from grinning, then started on the thirteen times, but didn't get beyond three times thirteen before she had to bury her face in another tissue.

In the kitchen, Cynthia began to bang the crockery around. 'Haven't you even got a coffee plunger?'

'Nope.' Ben didn't turn round. 'There isn't room for fancy things here.'

'You're telling me! It's a real hovel. I don't know what you see in it, I really don't! It's not as if you couldn't afford a decent place.'

'We love it here.' He exchanged a laughter-filled glance with his wife.

Suddenly Megan was feeling wonderful. Warmth seemed to be coursing through her veins. She beamed across at him and he grinned back, rolling his eyes in Cynthia's direction.

As she sipped the coffee, Megan felt happiness continue to surge through her. Far from being besotted with their guest, Ben seemed to be getting more irritated by her each minute. The fire was starting to burn well now and in the small room its warmth was soon felt.

But best of all was the warmth of her husband's gaze.

He came to perch on the arm of Megan's couch. She looked up at him. 'That's a lovely blaze. You're a dab hand with fires. I shall have to appoint you Lord of the Flames.'

He gripped her shoulder briefly. 'I shall be honored, milady.'

Megan could feel the familiar longing uncurl in her

belly. It seemed ages since they'd made love properly. If only Cynthia weren't there, she'd drag him into the bedroom right now! Or spread the blanket in front of the fire and tug him down to join her.

A sweetly acid voice broke the spell. 'I hate to interrupt you two love-birds, but what are we going to do about a meal tonight?'

Megan came reluctantly back to reality and her duties as a hostess. 'Did you bring back some steak?'

It was Ben who answered. 'Sorry. I forgot. I was - um, having a few other troubles.'

She bounced to her feet. 'Well, it won't take me long to whip up a spaghetti bolognese.' Something fell on her head and she looked up. 'Oh, no!' She pointed to the ceiling.

'Hell!' Ben stared up at the dripping water, whose rate had definitely speeded up. Several drips now formed a line across the middle of the ceiling.

Cynthia rolled her eyes. 'Look, why don't we all go into Bunbury? There's a rather nice hotel there. We can stay the night and travel back to Perth tomorrow.'

Ignoring her, Ben spoke to Megan, 'I'm going to have to do something about that leak, I'm afraid, or the furniture will be ruined. Keep the fire going, will you? I'll have to get up on the roof and stick a tar patch over the hole. Lucky someone left a half roll of tar paper here. I think it's still usable.'

He went over to the window, pulling a face at her over his shoulder. 'That rain's here to stay and it's going to be dark soon.'

She stood up. 'You'll need help.'

'You've only just got yourself warm.'

'So, I'll have to get warm again afterwards.' Their eyes met in a promise about how that warming would be accomplished.

'It won't take me long once I'm up there.' The wind whistled round the house and he added ruefully, 'Though it won't be much fun in this weather.'

Within minutes, he had the ladder leaning against the side of the house. With his hair plastered down by the driving rain, he had a sleek otter look about him, Megan thought dreamily.

She stood at the bottom of the ladder, making sure it didn't slip as he climbed on to the roof. He had a very nice backside, she decided, looking up. There was something distinctly sexy about damp, clinging jeans on a muscular male body.

He slipped and cursed as he found his footing again.

That jolted her out of her dreaminess. 'Be careful!' she warned him unnecessarily.

'Don't worry! I don't intend to get hurt!' He smiled down at her and she realised they were working as a team. That made her feel even better.

'You might as well stand under the shelter of the veranda until I'm ready to come down,' he called.

'I'd rather stay here and keep an eye on you. Besides, I'm already soaked. What's a little more rain between friends?'

He grinned down at her, and began to crawl across the roof. She stood watching him, her heart in her mouth. Surely that wind was getting stronger? After a few minutes, she could not help asking, 'Are you certain you're all right up there?'

'Never better!'

'Some sunburned country this is!' She tried to match his cheerfulness, but shivered as the wind blew moisture into every opening in her clothes and cold rain started to trickle down her neck. The wind seemed to be getting stronger by the minute.

She watched him investigate the leak and listened incredulously as he began to whistle. But the same happiness was welling up in her. 'You know, this is fun, in a backhanded sort of way,' she called out. 'We only need Gene Kelly to start us off and we'll be dancing - and singing - in the rain.' She sang the words of the song to him.

He sat up for a moment to ease his back. 'You're incredible. There you are, cold, soaked to the skin, yet you're managing to smile and joke, and you're even serenading me.'

'Well, you're whistling.'

'I think we're both mad.'

'I know we're mad!' He turned back to his work and the whistling started again.

'Megan!' Cynthia peered out of the door. 'Where's Ben?'

'Up on the roof.'

'Well, that bucket needs emptying again and I'm not touching it.'

'You'll have to, or it'll overflow all over the floor and then you'll get your nice new Reebocks wet.'

'You come and do it, then.'

'As you can see, I'm holding the ladder and I daren't let go.' Megan choked back a laugh at the expression of fury on Cynthia's face.

As the door was banged shut, her smile faded, however, and she stared back up at the roof. Heavy rain was slashing sideways across the darkening landscape, so strong was the wind now. 'How's it going?' she called, needing to hear his voice.

'Nearly finished. It's only a temporary repair, but it should hold for a day or so till this rainy spell is over, then I'll get someone in to fix the roof properly.'

Five minutes later he eased himself up into a half crouching position and threw his tools down onto the soft earth beside her. 'Hold that ladder steady.'

But he never got to the ladder. As he edged across the roof, an even stronger gust of wind screamed across the block, sucking up debris and leaves. Megan was thrown backwards onto the ground. The ladder thumped against the front of the house then spun away into the darkness.

She watched helplessly, unable to move for a moment.

The wind pinned her down, whirled debris about and lashed the trees into a frenzy. She was still watching as it caught Ben and made him lose his footing. He came bumping down the roof, yelling and clutching in vain at the flimsy guttering as he fell off the edge. He yelled even more loudly as he landed on the ground, then his voice cut off with terrifying suddenness.

As he lay there still and silent, terror filled Megan. She tried to go to him, but couldn't move a step, only moan his name helplessly. The wind shrieked round her like a demented torturer, lashing stinging rain and debris into her face. She could only clutch the wooden veranda post and pray he'd be all right.

Then, as suddenly as it had begun, the freak wind dropped and the rain started falling straight down again, showing in a pale curtain against the lights of the shack. Megan jumped to her feet and rushed across to Ben, who was lying ominously still with one leg bent under him. Dropping to her knees beside him, she felt the pulse in his neck, breathing a sigh of relief as his eyes flickered open. 'Don't try to move yet! You may have hurt your spine.'

He groaned and moved his head very gingerly to one side. 'I think it's my leg, not my back. Hurts like hell.'

By the light from the windows, Megan could see that he looked dazed.

'Keep as still as you can and I'll have a look.' Unfastening his shoe, she removed it to find his left ankle swelling fast and already showing dark mottled bruising. She straightened the leg as gently as she could, but he groaned as she touched it. Quickly she checked the rest of him. He had a gash on one cheek, but it was nothing serious, and there was a long shallow scrape on the back of one hand that was bleeding sluggishly.

'I think you may have broken your ankle.' She tried to keep her voice matter of fact.

'Mmm.' His face was a white blur in the darkness. 'You'll have to - drive to a phone - call an ambulance.'

'I'm not leaving you lying out in the rain. You'll get pneumonia.' She couldn't believe this had all happened so quickly and for a moment she had difficulty thinking what to do. 'What was that? A hurricane?'

'Just a sudden squall, I think.'

The front door opened and Cynthia peered out. 'What's hap - Oh!' She made no attempt to come outside.

'A freak wind blew Ben off the roof. We need to get him to hospital. You'll have to drive to the highway and find a phone.'

'Me? I can't.'

'What do you mean, you can't? I've seen you drive.'

'Yes, but not when I've had a drink or two. You weren't the only one who was chilled through today, you know. I've just had a couple of stiff gins to warm me up.'

'What does that matter?' Megan yelled, unable to believe that even Cynthia could be so selfish.

'They're murder on drink driving here in Australia. I've already lost my license twice for it. If you offend a third time, they put you in prison. So you'll have to drive for help while I stay here with Ben.' She made no effort to come out of the house, though.

Megan looked down at her husband, who had closed his eyes and was obviously in considerable pain. 'Stupid useless bitch!' she muttered. 'I'd like to throw her off the roof!'

Ben's hand came up to grasp hers. 'Join the club. I've been feeling like that all day. Nick shouldn't be so patient with her tantrums. She's far worse than she used to be.'

'I thought you were fond of her.'

'Hell, no! I was physically attracted to her once, but that didn't last long. I was sorry when Nick fell for her, but he was determined to marry her and he's old enough to know his own mind. I've just been trying to stop him worrying. He knows she drinks too much if she gets bored.'

He hesitated, then added, 'And he knows she's been

unfaithful to him, as well. Though not with me. I'd never do that to a friend, even if I still fancied her, which I don't.'

'Oh.' Megan sagged in relief. So all her jealousy had been unfounded. If he hadn't been in such pain, she'd have hugged Ben on the spot.

The wind had died right down but the rain was still falling steadily and she was chilled through. Blinking the water out of her eyes, she looked round, determination building up in her. 'If I drive for help, I'll have to leave you to Cynthia's tender mercies. I'm not doing that.'

'You've got no choice. I'm too big for you to carry.'

'There are two of us to carry you.'

'One and a half. Bet she's even weaker than she looks.' His grin changed quickly into a grimace. 'Ah, Megan, it hurts like hell!'

He was still clasping her hand and she bent her head to kiss his fingers quickly. 'Listen. I'm going to get you into the back of the station wagon and drive you to hospital. Moving you will hurt, but it'll be safer than leaving you here to die from exposure.' She raised her voice and bellowed, 'Cynthia!'

A figure appeared in the doorway.

'I need your help to lift Ben into the car.'

'Me?'

'Would you rather we left him lying here in the rain, you silly bitch? Come out here and help me at once.'

'How dare you speak to me like that!'

'Get out here at once or I'll drag you out by your hair, Cynthia Berevic!'

A shadow of a grin passed over Ben's face.

With Cynthia's reluctant help, Megan managed to get the station wagon backed up as close to her husband as possible. 'Go and fetch all the pillows and blankets off our bed, Cynthia. Oh, and while you're there, check whether the roof is still leaking. And hurry, will you!'

'This is the last time I ever come and stay with you two!

It's positively primitive here - roofs that leak, bathrooms like common wash houses, and not even a phone to call for help!'

Cynthia tottered to and fro, grumbling non-stop, while Megan piled the blankets and pillows in the car. Ben lay with his eyes closed, his face tense, but he was shivering now.

Megan bent over him. 'Ben, we need to get you into the car.'

His eyes gleamed briefly at her. 'Go ahead! I'll try not to . . . faint on you.'

'I know, love.' The endearment had slipped out without her noticing it, but he didn't seem to mind. For a moment, she thought she had heard him murmur, 'Dearest Megan,' but she couldn't be sure and now was not the time to ask him to repeat his words.

Two minutes later they were ready to lift him into the car. 'If you let go of him before I tell you to,' Megan hissed at Cynthia, 'I'll strangle you!'

'We're not all strapping country bumpkins like you!'

'Shut up and save what little strength you do have for the task at hand!'

In spite of the pain, Ben's lips twitched again, but as the two women lifted him up into the rear of the wagon, he moaned. And when Megan tried to arrange his foot so that driving wouldn't jar it too much, he fainted. She quickly took the opportunity to brace the foot with a second pillow.

'Go and get our handbags! And shut the door properly this time.' she ordered Cynthia. 'We'll have to drive him to the hospital. Do you know where the nearest one is?'

'No, of course I don't!'

'Then we'll drive towards Bunbury. It's closer than Mandurah.'

It seemed to take an eternity of bumping along the dirt track until they reached the highway. Megan ordered a protesting Cynthia to get out and open the gate, then close it. She drove carefully through it onto the hard shoulder at the side of the road, highly tempted to drive away and leave the other woman where she was, because Cynthia had not once stopped grumbling. Nor had she even tried to keep an eye on Ben in the back.

When they eventually found the hospital, she stopped at the emergency entrance, jumped out of the car and yelled for help. By the time two white-clad figures came out with a trolley she had the back door open, so that they could get to Ben.

Cynthia remained in the front seat, sobbing about how cold and wet she was.

Inside the medical team took Ben away and Megan allowed herself to be wrapped in blankets and fed a cup of stewed, but wonderfully hot tea by one of the nurses.

Someone must have coaxed Cynthia out of the car, because Megan could see her, similarly wrapped in blankets, at the other side of the room. She was still weeping over her cup of tea.

Megan didn't attempt to go over to her, because all her attention was on the door through which the stretcher had disappeared. It wasn't just his ankle; it was how chilled Ben had been that worried her.

When a doctor appeared, it was to confirm that her husband had indeed broken his ankle and would need to have it set under anaesthetic. 'He'll not recover consciousness for a while after that. Has he eaten recently? He hasn't? Oh, good, then we needn't wait to operate. Look, Mrs Saunders, you'd be better going home and telephoning in later for news.'

'We live on a country block and we aren't on the phone yet, so I'd rather wait here until I know he's all right.'

'As you wish.'

A nurse came up to her as the doctor left. 'You'll need to sign some forms, Mrs Saunders, then we have to get you and your friend warm. You're both shivering still.'

'She's no friend of mine!'

'I heard that!' Cynthia's tears ended abruptly and she glared at another nurse, who was standing beside her. 'I want a taxi calling, one that'll take me back to Perth. I'll pay for this stupid blanket or send it back or whatever. I'm not staying with that heartless harridan for one minute longer!'

She scowled across at Megan, 'And as for you and your husband, I hope you both catch double pneumonia. You've turned him into a stupid clod like yourself and I think the pair of you richly deserve one other. If I'd realised how besotted he was with his little Cinderella, I'd not have wasted my time with him. He used to be fun to know once!'

She stormed across to the nurses' desk. 'Have you got me that taxi yet?'

Megan sat there bemused, then a smile crept across her face. Besotted? Could Ben really be besotted with her? Cynthia seemed to think so.

Megan frowned, not quite daring to believe this. How could Cynthia know? Had he told her?

Suddenly she had to know. She ran across to the door and caught Cynthia's arm just as the other woman was stepping into a taxi. 'What do you mean by saying Ben's 'besotted' with me? Why did you say that?'

Cynthia tried to shake her off, but Megan wouldn't let go.

'Tell me!'

'Are you really too stupid to see how he looks at you? It's rather amusing, you know. The almighty Ben Saunders hooked at last – and by a nobody like you.'

She pushed her face closer to Megan's, almost snarling, 'It won't last, though. It definitely will not last. You're a novelty at the moment, but he'll soon get bored with your naiveté and your lost causes.'

Megan let go and stepped back, feeling joy run through her. 'I'll make very sure he doesn't, believe me. Go back and look after that nice husband of yours, for once.'

She didn't wait to see the taxi leave, but turned back into the hospital. Was Cynthia right? Did Ben indeed love her? What if she told him she loved him? Dare she do that? She drew in a deep breath, then nodded. Yes, she did dare. She must.

She couldn't go on like this, tiptoeing around her husband. Better a clean break than a lingering pain. Only - Cynthia had said 'besotted'. Oh, please, let that be true!

A nurse took the cup from her hands and said something. Megan blinked at her. 'Sorry! I was miles away.'

'I was just asking how you're feeling.'

'Better now. You've been very kind. Sorry Cynthia was so rude to you.'

'Oh, we're used to people like madam. You get all types here. Look, I've got my jogging gear in my locker. You and I are about the same size. I could lend you the track suit, then we could get you out of those wet clothes and dry them in the patients' laundry.'

Several hours later, the nurse woke Megan from her doze on a bench in the waiting area. 'Your husband's awake now, Mrs Saunders. He's a bit groggy, but he's asking for you.'

Megan threw off the blanket and followed her eagerly, sitting by the bed and holding Ben's hand. He seemed to have fallen asleep again, but she wanted very much to stay by his side.

'He'll be in and out of consciousness for a while.' The tired-looking nurse stopped for a moment at the foot of the bed. 'But I think he'll be happier to find you with him. I shouldn't let you up here at this hour, actually, but who's going to know?'

When Ben's eyes flickered open a little later, Megan leaned forward and said softly, 'I'm here, darling.'

He blinked and struggled to focus on her face. 'Megan? Is that you?'

'Yes. You've had an operation on your ankle. Everything's going to be all right.'

'So stupid, falling off the roof like that.' He sighed. 'Nothing you can do about sudden squalls, though. Megan – '

'Yes?'

'You were marvellous.'

'Well, I couldn't leave you lying out there on the ground in the middle of a storm, could I?' Had he not noticed her calling him darling? She'd been longing to do that for a while.

His eyes seemed to be in better focus now and he said quietly, as he gazed at her, 'You're beautiful.'

'I must look a real mess! The nurse lent me this and . . . '

His fingertips fluttered over her lips, stopping her speaking. 'Shh. I need to tell you something. Before I lose my nerve.'

She leaned closer, her heart suddenly speeding up to pound in her chest and her breath catching in her throat. 'What?'

'I love you, Megan.'

'Oh, Ben!' She slipped off the chair to kneel beside the bed and bury her head in his shoulder. 'I love you, too, but I thought you didn't believe in love and romance.'

His hand came up to caress her neck and face. 'Well, I've changed my mind. Are you quite sure you love me?'

'I'm very sure, darling.'

'Bad temper and all?'

'Every grouchy bit of you.'

He gave a long, happy sigh. 'That's so good to know.' His eyes closed again and his breathing slowed down.

A couple of hours later, just as dawn was brightening the room, he woke properly, seeming almost his normal self.

Megan, still sitting in the chair by his side, looked at him rather shyly.

He stretched out his hand to take hers. 'I did tell you I loved you, didn't I?'

'Yes, you did.' She felt suddenly breathless.

'Good. And did you tell me you loved me, too, or did I just dream that bit?'

She blushed. 'No. I do love you, Ben. Very much.'

His eyes held hers. 'I started falling in love with you that day in Edinburgh, I think - only I wouldn't admit it, even to myself. Hell, how could I ever have thought I had no need for romance? I need you quite desperately, dearest Megan. And I need our love, too.'

'I think it started with me that day, too.'

He pulled her towards him. 'You'd better give me a proper kiss, then, or I won't believe this is real.'

He pulled her towards him and as he began to kiss her, the magic flared again.

'Ben, darling,' she murmured, able at last to speak the words of love that had been dammed up inside her for the past few weeks.

'Dearest Megan, say you love me. I need to hear it again and again.'

'Of course I love you.'

'Don't ever change. I love you, too. In fact, I'm going to fill your life with so much love you'll not even notice there are other men in the world.'

'Are there really any others?'

He gave her one of his sexy looks. 'How soon can I go home? Go and tell that damned doctor I need to go home at once. We'll find some way to make love.'

'In a minute. Just lie there and rest for a while.'

Megan didn't attempt to get off the bed, but snuggled her head against his shoulder, sighing happily.

The miracle she'd longed for had occurred. She'd found love. And it had been well worth waiting for.

A few minutes later, she raised her head as a thought struck her. 'You know, your aunt's a very wise woman. She said we'd suit.'

'She's even wiser than I thought, then.'

'How could she tell we'd suit one another, though?'

'Feminine instinct. Who cares?' He felt a trickle of moisture on his hand and raised himself on one elbow. 'Now what's the matter with you, woman?'

She tried to sniff away the tears, but could not. 'I always cry when I'm happy, so you'll just have to get used to it. Unless you intend to make me unhappy.'

'No. So I shall have to get used to you weeping.' He stroked her hair, and as the tears wet his fingers, he chuckled in her ear. 'Stop that bawling at once and kiss me again, dearest - darling - Megan.'

A nurse glanced into the room, grinned, and left them alone again. No need to ask Mr Saunders if he was feeling better.

Printed in Great Britain
by Amazon.co.uk, Ltd.,
Marston Gate.